Jamie is a teacher who has studied a geography degree back in the nineties because of his love of nature and the outdoors. He found environmental education especially important and soon became a teacher for the primary-age group.

Jamie enjoys reading and watching all kinds of theatre productions, from high dramas to lively musicals. His love of writing shines through in everything he does.

For my mum, for always standing by me and
supporting me throughout.
For my nan, for looking after me when I was young and
showing me how to dream.

Jamie Adams

THE FATHERS, THE SONS AND THE ANXIOUS GHOST

AUSTIN MACAULEY PUBLISHERS™

LONDON • CAMBRIDGE • NEW YORK • SHARJAH

A CIP catalogue record for this title is available from the British Library.

ISBN 9781528917360 (Paperback)
ISBN 9781528961875 (ePub e-book)

www.austinmacauley.com

First Published (2019)
Austin Macauley Publishers Ltd
25 Canada Square
Canary Wharf
London
E14 5LQ

Table of Contents

Introduction to Characters

Matt is married to Hannah, and they have a son named Max.

Josh is a school teacher who is separated from his wife and has a son called Sam.

Alex is married to Michelle. They have a boy and a girl, Alfie and Tess.

Part One – The Fathers

Chapter 1 (Matt)

The rain was thundering down against the car bonnet. The window wipers were going at it but seemed to have no effect in clearing the cloudy windscreens. The clock read 8:20, and I knew we were going to be up against it if we wanted to make it to school in time. I blame her! We could have just sent him to the local primary school. It was just down the road. We could have practically fallen out of the front door and arrived at school each day. Instead of this, Hannah had to fight for a place at a school in the next town. She said it had better results. She reckoned it would far improve his chances of doing well in life and set him up well for secondary school. What a load of rubbish! All it did was put an eight-mile journey down single carriageway roads in between us and where he needed to go each day. A road which was winding and often blocked with farm vehicles and slow-moving buses, parked cars and the occasional horse. It was his special assembly today. I could not let him be late! Each year group only did one play a year, and this was going to be it for him; his big day.

She could not even be bothered to attend the thing. She had a meeting which she simply could not miss! I had arranged to go into work late, but she refused to change her meeting as she said it meant losing client confidence. Clients came first. At least that is how it seemed to me. She never changed her things around for me or him. Poor Max never moaned or whinged about it, but he must have known that she could have gone if she felt like it. Anyway, I clapped and made a fuss of him, regardless.

He bundled into the back seat, chucked his bag next to him and closed the door, shutting out the rain. I waited for him to click his seatbelt together and put my foot down. With any luck, we would make it in time, with moments to spare. His mother stood under the shelter of the porch way and smiled at him sweetly. How fake it all felt. She was probably working out who she could screw over today, and how much she could swindle them for. After all, lawyers are always thinking of their next win. They preyed on misfortunes and opportunities which usually arose out of conflict. Max wiped down his coat and then called out to me.

"Turn up the radio, Dad!"

Ed Sheeran was on. I knew exactly what this meant. He started to join in with the lyrics. I soon joined in as well. Before long, being late had slipped my mind. We belted out the song and swayed our heads in time with the beat. He punched the air periodically, and I beeped the horn at the end of the chorus.

"I love it when we do that, Dad."

The local countryside had quickly passed us by. We were now entering the neighbouring town and seemed to be doing well. As the radio blurted out the news, I began to become aware of how much my thighs hurt me right then. It had been a tiring 'leg day' at the gym the night before.

So many people thought I was one of those gym obsessives. I wasn't. I admit it made me feel good. Well…it made me feel good afterwards at least. When the endorphins have been released, and you have worked up a sweat, your body automatically feels relaxed; and stress is relieved a bit, even if momentarily. The main reason I started going was to give me some space from HER. I did it to get me out of the house. Originally it was just twice a week, but now it was almost every day. Addiction?! Not really. Avoidance tactic?! Yes – that is a better way of describing it.

I may have avoided her more than ever lately, but I needed to make sure Max knew I was always there for him. That was the point of today. I had booked the morning off from work especially to watch his Easter play. He had asked me to several times, so I had to make sure I came. Even though his rehearsals at home had been a bit uncomfortable, he couldn't help it. She put his nerves on edge. Some people said he had speech and language issues, but I could see that was not the case. When he was comfortable, he spoke crisply and could get across his points clearly. He was happy to share his opinions with me. We had great chats and I loved when we did car karaoke. The stuttering always subsided a bit when he began to sing.

Anyway, here we were. Parking was a nightmare, but we had made it with minutes to spare. I walked him into the atrium, and he told me he was looking forward to it but was afraid he might screw up his lines. I reminded him that he was going to get a KFC treat after school as a reward for working so hard. He kissed me, and I sought out a seat. Just as I sat down, I noted Alex just a few places along. He nodded at me in a cool but nondescript way. I returned the nod subtly and tried to get myself comfortable on one of those awful plastic, far-too-small chairs. I wondered if Alex's boy had got a chance to be seen by that footie scout. Or was it just bullshit? Even when we were teenagers, I could never tell when the bullshit ended and the truths began… Not when it came to Alex. He was a good guy, but something made me think he fantasised too much. I guess being stuck with a cow like her, he had to have a good imagination to keep himself sane. Hmm. Where was she today? Not like her to miss a school event.

Lights went off. Lights went on. Oh, there was that teacher again. Max thought he was amazing. His speech was short and sweet. Fingers were crossed. I glimpsed Max looking a cross between pumped up and on a knife edge. I hoped he would try and enjoy the show.

Chapter 2 (Josh)

All he cared about was buffing up, toning his muscles and eyeing himself up in the mirror. I knew this because you could sometimes catch him glimpsing himself in the camera of his phone, as if about to take a selfie. We all knew what he was doing. He was checking his form. Was self-obsessed. What a brute! If only I had time to go to the gym more. Then I could beef up like him. Instead, I just looked slender; a bit awkward and flimsy in comparison.

Marking books was my time consumer. Every night I spent nearly two hours catching up on marking maths and English books, tweaking my lesson plans and adapting smart notebooks ready for the following day. Every day we lived in fear of observations, book scrutinies and inspections. We had no choice but to work all evening, every evening, just to keep afloat. That is why being a separated father was so hard for me to handle. Teaching does not fit well with bringing up a child. Luckily, the mum and I got on well. We had split many years ago and never really fell out. She just knew that being in a relationship was not right for me. Well…not with a woman at any rate. Although I am not sure if she knew deep down that I was gay.

Part of me thought I would end up married one day and just tow the line and be straight like everybody else. For now, I just threw myself into work and hoped for the best. I wanted to become a head teacher one day and maybe, just maybe, even make a difference in the world of education. At least I was on track. My boss liked me. I had some responsibilities at work. My kids kept on making good progress. I just needed to keep my head nice and clear. I needed to keep away from the 'Tinder' app. I needed to mark and plan and work and drive forward so that I didn't get dragged into that sordid world of dating apps and pointless hook-ups. I could manage all of that. Well…some distractions just kept on creeping in.

Anyway, he rushed in, having a few words of encouragement for his son before his big moment. I could see his perfect teeth shining, and his hair unmoving in the breeze that the half-held open doorway was creating. I collected my class together sheepishly, marking them off on the register and ushering them towards my TA, who stood, supportively, keeping them calm and getting them settled into the right places. Max raced up to me, excited. I hoped that he could keep control of his nerves and get the speech out. Hopefully, with his dad in the background, he could pull it out of the bag.

The hall was filling up quickly and the head teacher came over to talk to me about whether or not the children were going to go over to their parents afterwards for a hug and chat. She seemed to think it was better if the kids just took their applause and then left the hall before the parents could get up. That way, there was no chance of losing anyone. Everyone was a bit on edge, as a school child in a neighbouring village had been abducted by his criminal father just a week ago. I accepted her instructions and sat down with my script, ready to prompt anyone who forgot their lines. Suddenly the lights went off, and then there was an awkward moment while they found the switch to make the stage lights fade in. As the lights focused, I returned my fix on his outline. His body looked radiant in the half light, with his muscles clearly defined; and his chiselled chin striking in the distance, standing out amongst the melee of the largely feminine crowd. I do not know why he intrigued me so much. I resented him to a large extent, but, in spite of that, I somewhat admired him.

As I stood there, the crowd hushed, and my heartbeat seemed audible. I looked at the class and could see their excitement bubbling. A few looked a little sick but still keen. The thing with kids is they often cannot control their emotions. Excitement leads to nerves. Nerves can lead to unpredictable bursts of vomiting. I took a deep breath and went for it.

"Good morning, everybody."

The whole school replied, "Good morning, Mr Johnson."

"Welcome to the Ravens class spring assembly."

Off we went. No stopping us now…

Chapter 3 (Alex)

"Mummm!"

I wished he would give it a rest.

"Dadddd!" he went on.

It made me wonder why his mum never answered. I was too busy trying to get knots out of Tess' hair.

"What's wrong now?" I replied anxiously.

Alfie stormed in with a red face and swollen, angry cheeks.

"I can't find my football socks anywhere!" he announced.

"Try under the bed," I said, trying to remain calm and de-escalate his crossness.

"Ouch," squirmed Tess softly, as I caught yet another knot.

She was always so relaxed. She never let anything get to her. She was ten times cooler than Alfie, whose hot-headedness got him into scrapes—left, right and centre.

He stormed out again and slammed the door to his room. I winced and hoped that he could find those damn socks, or we would never hear the end of it. The clock was staring at me and reminding me that we hadn't got much time left. I went to find Michelle.

The distant noise of a bath filling, coupled with an aroma of scented steam made it obvious that she would not be coming this morning. When we woke up this morning, she told me that she had had a bad night's sleep, and her headache was back. Women use headaches as excuses to get out of things, but this was not like her! She always liked to be involved in school-related stuff. She loved the banter between mums. Her favourite thing was pricking her ears up and listening intently for any titbits of gossip that she could soak up from the gaggle of parents, who would usually surround her on that packed and bustling playground. Maybe this time she was actually feeling a bit sick. Quickly I realised I should attend to this in a sympathetic, understanding way. After all, she had cared for me, like a private nurse, when I had man flu last Christmas.

"Are you alright?" I tried, gently.

She turned off the tap to the bath and opened the window slightly to let out some steam.

"Have fun today. I bet the assembly goes well."

I could tell she was not feeling very well. She kept holding her head; sort of wiping her brow as she spoke. I had not seen her look like this for a long, long while. Thinking back, I should have realised that this was out of the ordinary for her. Instead of prying further, I left her to it, planting a quick kiss on her forehead and then rushing down the stairs.

Alfie and Tess soon followed, and we collected our things and burst out into the driveway, where they ran to the car; Alfie calling shotgun as usual to make sure he got to sit in the front passenger seat. I asked if he had kissed his mum, and he simply said the bathroom door was shut. Tess went on to say, "I hope Mummy gets better soon because I want to go swimming later."

When we got Tess off to class, and I had signed Alfie in, I went to find a seat next to someone I barely knew and sent Michelle a text. Quickly I switched off the phone and tucked my coat under my chair. I gave a slight nod to Matt as he rolled in, just in time. The lights came on and that teacher did the introduction. It did not cross my mind that today was going to turn out so black and dismal and full of anger.

Chapter 4 (Matt)

The thing with school assemblies these days is they tend to combine the classes together, so you end up with 60 kids in each performance, taken from two classes. It meant that lots of kids had non-speaking parts. That is why I was grateful for Max getting a chance to say some lines.

The whole production was quite basic but effective. It told the story of the life of Roald Dahl, and they had cleverly changed some pop songs to fit in nicely. Someone had decided to take the old Pussycat Dolls song from back in the day, *Don't Cha*, and make it fit with a scene about George and his marvellous medicine. It went something like, "Dontcha think my medicine's so good, Grandma. Dontcha think my medicine's the best... By far..." It made me laugh, and I admit Alfie did a good job as George. He kind of always looked a bit menacing anyway, so that role suited him well.

A few kids screwed up their lines or forgot to bring the right thing onto stage at the right time, but generally, it was quite a good laugh. I wanted Max to get on and do his bit, so he could take it easy again. I spotted him sitting quietly and looking awkward just below the edge of their worn-out stage. Several times I tried to catch his attention, but he was glued to his script, following each line and, no doubt, re-learning his words again. I remembered hating being in school plays and doing everything I could to get out of having a speaking part. I usually managed to wangle being the props boy or hiding as one of the boys in the crowd. Max definitely always faced his fears head on. My eye was caught by a little kid telling a joke about one of Roald's friends being beaten repeatedly by the headmaster when, awkwardly, Max strolled on.

It was just all of a sudden. He quickly shot up from his place and crossed the stage in long striding movements. I could see that the others had not quite finished their scene yet. They looked at him oddly. He opened his mouth to speak. Alfie, who was on stage as a 'naughty boy from Roald Dahl's class', whispered something to Max menacingly and gave him a nudge. Max looked embarrassed as he realised he had timed it wrong. As he stepped back, he flipped backwards onto the floor. It all seemed to be happening in slow motion. It did not seem to be real; more of a vision than a real sequence of events. I could see that he had tripped over another boy's foot. As he fell, his other leg flicked out and caught Alfie in the shin. The other boy yelled as most of the top-half of Max landed on him awkwardly. It was all kicking off now.

Instantly, Alfie swung a fist at Max, and I knew I had to go up there and help him. Alex rushed up to the stage too, and we ended up having to hold the boys back from each other. The boy who had been crushed had also got up and was pushing both of them. Quickly the teacher grabbed him and told him to go back to the class room. My heart was racing. That bloody git, Alfie, had given my boy a black eye. I just about managed to hold back the swearing until we had been able to drag them all back into the corridor, away from the ears of that group of vultures gossiping in that packed, sweaty school hall.

I lost my rag a bit. I told that Alfie's dad what I thought of him. Alex just shouted back at me a lot. He reckoned my son had screwed up the whole play. I lifted my arm up in what seemed like slow motion, about to make a move towards him with my clenched fist. Before I had had time to follow through, I felt someone grab my wrist. Alex ducked anyway and stepped back as the teacher pulled my arm down and asked me to take a few minutes outside while he quizzed the boys to find out what had gone wrong. I had to assume the play just carried on, as the rest of the school building seemed barren and deserted still.

When I got out into the fresh air, I took a deep breath and started to wish that I smoked. My blood was boiling. I could not face the other parents knowing, or thinking they knew, that my son had messed up this Easter production. God knows what the Missus would say. No doubt she would blame it on me, as usual. My legs caved, and I sank to the floor, back against the wall, knees bent. Alex must have found somewhere else to hide. I was glad he was not around, or I would have been tempted to knock his block off at that moment.

After what seemed like days, the teacher finally came and found me. He asked if I wanted a cup of tea and explained that the head teacher was discussing everything with the boys.

"Sorry that happened," Mr Johnson began, calmly.

"It's not your fault," I growled, slightly easing up as I spoke.

"Well, I can only apologise for my son. His foot got in the way," he carried on, still very pleasant and genuine.

"Oh shit. That was your boy. Is he alright?"

"Just a bruised ego. Your boy has a bruise developing near his eye. We have put a cold compress on it, and it seems to be reducing the swelling."

"Let me see Max."

"You can, I just need you to promise you will act calmly around school. I do understand your reaction though."

"Thanks. I was a bit hot-headed, but it ain't nice seeing your boy getting beaten up."

He walked me into the head's office, and she offered me a chair.

Chapter 5 (Alex)

I could see Matt going into her office and tried to avert making eye contact, as I knew he would be nasty. Alfie was still sat in a chair slumped over a table in the Year One classroom. He was angry, crying and refusing to talk to me. His stubbornness always ruled him during times like these. I paced up and down with my hands behind my back and thought about calling his mum. No... I needed to man up! I needed to handle this one myself and show him how to deal with his emotions. She would just soften to him in order to calm him down and give him treats to take his mind off of it. Sometimes he would speak to her like a piece of dirt on the sole of his shoes. If only I had been stronger and waded in more in the past, we might not have let it get this far. I mean I would always stick up for him. Don't get me wrong, I loved my son. If only he could learn to tow the line and settle down more rather than losing his rag all the time.

"Look mate... We really need to deal with this. I don't want you going home and upsetting your mum (oh why did I say that?). Let us go through this together."

He shrugged and sniffed a lot; the kind of snotty sniff that resonates around the room.

"What made you do it, mate?" I tried being sensitive and put my hand on his shoulder.

He brushed it away and wriggled a bit.

"I don't blame you! I just want to understand what went through your head, mate."

"Stop calling me mate!" he finally responded snappily, yet surprisingly without shouting.

I paced around some more and started to wonder whether Tess saw any of this. She must have done as the whole school was watching. I hoped she was alright. Mind you, the kids had not even come back from the assembly yet. Suddenly I heard what must have been a round of applause. It sounded like they had completed the play after all and now were about to return to their rooms. I needed to get him out of here so as not to create a scene with the other children.

"We need to get out of the class now. The Year Ones will be on their way back."

"Who cares!?" he whimpered, with his eyes still closed.

"We don't want the little ones to worry about you, do we!?" I pointed out carefully.

It was too late. They suddenly started coming into the room, and the teaching assistant clocked us and asked me to take Alfie into the reception area. She ushered the Year Ones silently onto the carpet, ready for the teacher to follow. The teacher was a small-framed woman, who looked quite unimpressed by the situation. Her eyes glared at me, with a stern message underlining their discomfort.

I took Alfie's hand and practically dragged him out of that room. I did not want her to start a scene. Although, to be honest, that teacher's stare that she gave me went right through my bones. It somehow instantly reminded me of my own childhood and that scary teacher who used to stand over us when we did exams, looking down at us through her sharply polished glasses. I had always been pretty well-behaved, but part of that was down to the fear of what she might do. Her stare always seemed calculating and menacing. She seemed to spend her time scanning for trouble. Luckily, I never got on the wrong side of her, but the fear was still there. This Year One teacher had that same evil stare. Penetrating.

Alfie kept relatively quiet as he hitched his way down the corridor with me still attached. Part of me wondered if they would consider me a bad parent for doing this; but when I glanced back over my shoulder, I could see the relief in the face of the teaching assistant who moments earlier had looked startled.

The head teacher had come to look for us by now, and we were taken back to her room; which was to my surprise, empty. She closed the door peacefully and proceeded to sit down at her desk, taking her hair band off as she did, releasing a full head of mousey brown hair.

"Max has been taken to hospital as a precaution. It seems he has had quite a bad headache ever since the incident, and he has bruising around his right eye."

"I can only apologise for everything today, Mrs Bellamy," I murmured, reading the name badge on her blouse because I could never recall her surname.

"I think I need to hear what Alfie has to say about all of this," she went on.

"Alfie takes a while to think about what he has done, before he can talk much about it, miss," I replied.

"I am married, sir," she uttered and then carried on with her attempts to goad a response from Alfie. "Look at me, young man! This is not the first time that you have hurt someone at school."

I tried to change the subject. "I do hope Max is OK. How badly do you think he is hurt?" I queried.

"Alfie, can you pick your head up for me and look at me? I need to make sure you are alright as well," she continued, regardless of my attempts to ease her off.

"I can tell that he is very sorry, Mrs Bellamy. He rarely cries like this, so he must be feeling bad."

"He can cry as much as he likes, but he needs to face up to things, sir," she replied, snappily.

"I won't do it again, miss," he murmured.

"I am going to have to think about what happens next, but for now I am sending you home to contemplate your actions," she replied sternly.

I took him by the hand, and he reluctantly went with me back to the car. He was in a right state, and I was not sure that going home right now would go down well. I decided to take him down to the beach and have a proper chat with him before going into work. In fact, as I drove along through the busy streets, with the radio blaring, I decided to text in to work when we parked and give myself the day off. If he could be naughty, so could I after all. We pulled up at the car park by the beach, and I got him to go and put change into the pay machine. For some reason, he liked doing this. To be honest, he had slightly cheered up now that we were away from his school. I had to make sure he learned his lesson and didn't just have a doss day while his poor school friends were stuck in classrooms, reciting times tables.

Chapter 6 (Josh)

What a day! What a shit day that was! I usually love my work, but today really took the piss. I was so glad to finally be home; with the TV on, Sam buried in his bedroom with a shoot-'em-up game exploding in the background, and the dog whimpering for his feed by my calves. Everything was back to normal; at least for now. Maybe an episode of 'Suits' could take my mind off of it. Then later on, I would be able to quiz Sam a bit more about what had happened earlier.

Bugger. The phone rang. I pondered just ignoring it, but I knew it would only ring again. It was the house phone, which was unusual. I dragged my feet across the living room until I could just about reach the handset. "Hello mate." It was Conor. What a relief. Conor had been my best friend since the 90s and was always fun to be around.

"Fancy drowning your sorrows?" He carried on, quickly.

How could I turn him down? It was probably just what the doctor ordered.

"See you at the Crown in ten," I replied, popping the phone down, sliding my slippers off and marching towards the bedroom to find some deodorant.

I nipped past Millie's room and asked her to keep an eye on Sam for me. Millie was a great housemate, as she was always around and willing to look after Sam, especially when I needed some light relief. Millie and Sam got along well anyway. She was a PhD nerd, studying molecular biology; and he was a kid who was crazy about animals and wildlife shows. They would often sit glued to one of those epic David Attenborough series on the telly. Sam rushed up to me and gave me a hug and then asked if he could steal a piece of treacle tart from the fridge. I agreed, and he went on his way, scooping up the dog as he skipped.

When I arrived at the pub, Conor wasn't there yet. Typical. He was always late. Even though he was the one that said to be there in ten. I may as well have added half an hour to anything he said. Mind you, he didn't expressly say ten minutes. He could have meant ten days or ten weeks or even ten years. What could I do? I hated being in a pub alone. I grabbed a Jack Daniels from the bar and wandered over to the quiz machine to try my luck on one of those movie quizzes where you win a quid if you answer ten questions correctly. I was soon absorbed in it and ran out of change. As I turned to switch a tenner for some one pound coins, I felt a strong hand on my shoulder.

As I stopped and turned, it all seemed to go into slow motion. The hand was attached to a muscular arm, upon which sat an expensive-looking watch. Soon that dark, perfectly combed hair appeared and those piercing, deep blue eyes. I was not expecting it to be him!

"Fancy seeing you here," he said, brightly.

"Hello again, I do hope your son is doing well," I replied, nervously.

I was not sure how Max had got on at the hospital but assumed that if Dad was here, he must've been relatively OK. I could smell a distinctive stench of the alcohol on his breath though, which could have simply meant he was drowning his sorrows.

"It's a long story; why don't you come and play pool, and I can tell you the details."

"Well, I am waiting to meet my friend, but he is running late. Suppose I can have a go, but I am not really any good at it," I wriggled as I stepped over to the pool table, and he put some coins in and retrieved a set of shiny yellow and red balls.

"How about you break then? Then you get to decide your own colour."

I grabbed a cue and tapped some chalk into the end of it frantically. A small dust cloud surrounded me, and I sneezed a bit as it tickled my nose. This was not going to be a relaxing evening after all. I was now playing a game that I was crap at against a guy that made me blush. Worst of all, this guy was a parent at the school I taught at, and his kid had been in a scuffle with mine that very morning! This had no chance of ending with anything other than humiliation.

He had made a neat, perfectly formed triangle with the balls, using one of those plastic frames. He tossed me the white. I just about caught it and circled the table in such a way that I might convince him I was eyeing up possible break shots, but actually I found myself doing everything not to lay my eyes on his face and study those distinct cheek bones and subtle dimples that made him look so chiselled and appealing. Whenever he turned his back, I would be eyeing him up rather than looking for opportunities to make a stunning first break of the balls and put him on the back footing.

I finally opened up the game with a reasonable break and got a yellow in before handing the table over to Matt. He was a little better than me but not nearly as good as I thought he would be. He took swigs of beer whilst lining up the balls and started to banter with me, just before I took a shot in order to put me off. I found myself loosening up and having some fairly successful shots at the balls.

I was quite involved in the game when Conor suddenly appeared in the background. He asked if Matt or I wanted a drink, and I took him up on it.

"No, but thank you," said Matt, politely.

"I will. It is the least you could do! If I were you, Matt, I'd take advantage of the fact he has his wallet open. Give it a chance for the bats to fly off and the cobwebs to blow away."

He apologised for being late and, being competitive, demanded to take on the winner of our game.

"Winner stays on. Loser buys next round," he said, cheekily.

Conor was always good at banter. He was always great at cheering people up. I could not ask for a better best mate. Matt soon joined in with a back and forth of random chat and we played on, swilling the drinks back.

I was just making my way back from the toilet when Conor sauntered over to me and ushered me into a booth for a chat. I knew immediately that something serious must have happened. His eyes were a little swollen, and his breathing had changed.

"I have to tell you this here. Matt has gone to get a round, and I was just checking my Facebook…" he said, awkwardly.

"Oh no! What has happened?" I said, sitting down for a moment. Conor shuffled towards me, secretively.

"Emily just sent me a message to say that police and ambulances are around Alex's house. It is all kicking off. It looks as if someone has died."

I could not believe my ears.

"Who died? Seriously?"

"Alex's wife…what's her name?"

"Oh shit! No way!"

"She doesn't know the details, but she saw them take a body away tonight," he retorted, quietly, as if trying to avoid being overheard. Ironically, just as he said this, a large hand grasped his shoulder and another presented him with a drink. Matt joined us with a slim-looking girl holding the other drinks, including mine.

The girl was blonde, about our age but maybe younger and looked very intelligent, with a long, flowing skirt and neatly tied back hair.

"Nicole just told me something bad has happened. You won't believe it."

The girl sat next to us and began to tell us what we already knew. It turned out that Nicole was Matt's cousin, and she was friends with Emily and had already spoken to Matt about the events unfolding. To my surprise, Matt was completely sympathetic.

"I wouldn't wish that upon anyone, mate," he murmured, gently. He had calmed down and was displaying a more serious side to his character.

I glimpsed the time and made my excuses before putting my coat on and waving them goodbye. I left Conor and Matt discussing today's events and Nicole finishing her drink swiftly before following me to the door. She seemed interested in my thoughts about Alex and his wife. I assured her that I knew very little about them other than that the wife was always at school events and seemed friendly, personable and always in good spirits. It seemed everything was not as clear cut as I had imagined.

Nicole soon went her separate way and gave me a hug before doing so. I weaved my way back through the hilly streets of my quaint little village, wondering how Matt would get home. I had genuinely wanted to get to know him; and despite his tough exterior, he had presented a side to himself which seemed passionate and warm. I pondered for a minute what it would be like to spend time alone with him and even to just feel his warm embrace.

As I flung open the door, Sam was in my face, asking me why all of his friends were messaging about trouble around at Alfie's, and whether or not it was true that Michelle was now dead.

Chapter 7 (Alex)

I kicked the ball over to him. He had started to loosen up a bit. He gave me a quick cheeky look and then booted the ball past my left shoulder and between the two rolled up jumpers that acted as goal posts. When he was playing footie, he was always much more himself. It allowed him to let off steam, and he really seemed to have a passion for it. I kind of hope this passion came from me. When I was his age, I had joined a team too; and we played every weekend, with my father as the coach. Maybe I could get him to open up a bit while we pounded the ball across the beach.

I tried to start a conversation with him a few times, but it never developed until we had a break and sat down with two large flake ice creams on the nearby park bench. We had both eaten them within seconds and sat side by side, staring at the empty beach.

"You know I didn't mean to hurt him," Alfie calmly announced.

"I know you didn't, mate."

"I just get so frustrated with him."

"What do you mean?" I wanted more details but tried not to be interrogating.

"Sometimes he takes soooo long to say what he wants to say. Sometimes he bugs me for ages, and I just don't know what he is on about," he went on.

"I see…" I was trying to be passive here.

"He can be friendly and stuff, but he is just so boring. I don't like how long he takes to do everything. He bores most of us."

"But you do like him deep down? Maybe he just wants to be your friend?" I tried to counsel him quietly.

"It's like Mum. She is always so soft and timid and boring. I love her, but she is never much fun to be around."

"I won't have you speak about your mum like that!" I snapped as the conversation suddenly hit a raw nerve.

"I just mean he is dull. He collects comics. I mean…who even reads comics these days!?"

"It is good to enjoy something like that." I took some deep breaths and got back to being reasonable.

"Mum does the same…her stuffed owls are everywhere." His eyes were down, looking at a small crab which seemed to have crawled from nowhere and was journeying diligently across the sand in front of us.

I tried to be clever and link our chat to this.

"Crabs have a lot to deal with, you know…" I went for it. "They have huge pincers and strong shells. They have to carry these around with them, which makes them quite slow and tempting for animals that want to eat 'em. They just want to get from one place to another and guzzle their food and hang out in rock pools."

"Dad, you are stupid, you know," he laughed out loud and with some raucousness.

I had not seen him laugh so freely in a while. It was a welcome release.

"It is just like us. We carry lots of crap on our shoulders, and all we want to do is eat, sleep and chill out." I started to laugh back at him, as sometimes watching him laugh full pelt made it impossible not to join him.

"You know, I may be stupid, but I am also your dad and always will be," I reminded him and gave him a head lock, brushing his head with my fingers to tickle him reassuringly.

He swung one arm around me and clutched me tightly, causing me to let go.

"I do love you," he nudged his face against me and rubbed cheeks before we happily sat watching the crab, reminiscing to the sound of the large waves crashing against the deserted pebbles. Still we had no idea of what was to come.

Chapter 8 (Matt)

When I got in she wasn't even there. The neighbour, George, was sat, watching the telly; and his wife was in the kitchen, boiling the kettle. It was 11:00 p.m.

"Hello, did you have a nice evening?" George enquired politely. "Ruby has got the tea on for you."

"I had no idea you were babysitting. If I had known, I would have come back earlier."

"Oh, don't worry, mate. She got called out with work, so we came around for a bit," Ruby replied, happily.

"Called out by who?" I asked, with some bewilderment.

"Work. Apparently they have a big case on tomorrow and need to go over their questions," George said, calmly.

"So what time did she leave?" I asked, innocently.

"About half an hour after you went down the pub," Ruby mumbled as she came in with a quivering tray of tea and cakes.

She wobbled so much that some of the tea overflowed onto the tray, nearly drenching the cakes.

I could not understand why she had not even texted me about it.

"It all seemed such a rush, so last minute…a bit urgent to be honest," Ruby carried on as she mopped up some of the drink with a towel.

"We made Max go to bed though. It was nice to get to read him a story," said George, with a satisfied look shining across his face.

"Well, I am really grateful, but it all seems a bit strange to me."

As I said this, messages began to come through on WhatsApp, as my wireless reconnected. It turned out she had messaged me several times, but I had had no signal at the pub, as usual. She had told me that she had to go and meet Kevin and Kim and go through some new evidence relating to their court appeal tomorrow. At least she wasn't being sneaky. Although I still reckoned that she could have tried texting me normally or even giving me a ring. I was beginning to think that she spent so much time apparently at work that surely there must have been more to it. Right now though, my mind was elsewhere.

I checked my own Facebook page and found a few people gossiping about the Alex thing. I noticed that Nicole had sent me a message to say that it was all true. Michelle had apparently passed away, and the police cars were still there. I wanted to message Alex but realised I would be the last person he would want to speak to right now. My mind changed again as I saw the 'people you may know' streak straddled across my home page. It was as if the computer had known that I had just met up with that teacher, Josh. It was suggesting we had mutual friends, and I found myself just clicking it, requesting him as a new contact. I assumed if other people had him on their Facebook, then he would be up for connecting to me as well. My mind skipped back to the matter we were concentrating on. I searched the local news website and low and behold there was an article about a suspicious death in the locality. Police at this stage were apparently just making enquiries and not ruling anything out.

I stumbled upstairs towards the toilet and peaked into Max's room where he was fast asleep. He had had a difficult day, and it struck me that his mother probably didn't spend any time with him before she left for work again. Part of me always felt that she was not right to be a mum. She was so moody. So uninterested. I often thought to myself that I must have been on drugs or something when I agreed to marry the bitch. Funnily enough, she had asked 'me' to marry 'her'. To be honest, I am not sure that I would have stuck with her if she had not trapped me by telling me she was pregnant with Max.

He was worth it all though. He was always well behaved and grateful for anything we gave him. Max was polite and thoughtful and never really moaned about much at all. That is except for the fact that he worried a lot. He was a worry wart. He would spend all his spare time scratching his head and thinking about stuff. Anything and everything would get to him. I just wished I could make him relax more and not take things too personally.

There was one time when we visited a zoo, and he was in such a great mood. He was laughing, and we were doing monkey impressions; his mother even joining in momentarily. We got as far as the giraffes, and one of them came towards him. He thought it wanted to meet him. His face was grinning from ear-to-ear.

Suddenly it lurched. Its foot was caught on a rock, and it leaned forward before stumbling and kneeling to the ground. It looked as though it had hurt its knee, and Max was horrified. I remember seeing the colour drain from his skin. His lips looked grey, and his face was the colour of ashen.

It took us about 15 minutes to pick him up off the floor and get him back to normal. A lot of coaching was needed…and chocolate. He worried about that poor giraffe every day since. I even sometimes found him logging onto the zoo website, trying to establish if the beast was still alive or not. He assured me it was! I dreaded the day when it wouldn't be!

My mind flashed back to that time we do not speak of. As I saw my little boy laying there peacefully, I remembered being younger, being excited about the future. The dark times that came over us after that would always leave a mark on me. I had to shake those thoughts away, as sometimes they could eat me up inside, especially at night time. I really did need to focus on the positives. I was a 'together' kind of person, and right now I must keep everything together…for Max's sake at least.

When I got out of the toilet, my phone screen lit up with a notification that Josh had accepted my friend request. I found myself instantly dropping him a message to say thanks for adding me back. Ruby kissed me on the cheek as she left, and George gave me a thumbs up in that 'old man' kind of way. I put my head on the cushion of the settee and changed channels on the telly until I came across a cheesy late-night show about dating on a tropical island. Just as my eyes started to tire, a message came up on Facebook, and I was alert again.

Chapter 9 (Josh)

As I lay there watching couples do ridiculous tasks on some Spanish island to test their relationships, I was surprised to see his message flick across the screen of my mobile. I reached out to check it and saw that he was thanking me for the add. I was about to put my phone down again when I suddenly felt the urge to check through his photos. Why couldn't I just leave it alone? After all, he was the parent of one of the kids in my class. Regardless, I flicked across several pictures of him on holiday and doing things with Max. After scanning through a few photo albums, I began to realise that he really had very few pictures of him and her. In fact, apart from a few formal occasions where she was in the picture by mistake or was in a group shot, he really had left her out of the albums altogether. It was like she didn't matter to him. Or maybe she just took all of the photos herself, and that is why she wasn't in front of the camera, but it still seemed peculiar to me.

I wondered what tomorrow would be like. The death was going to create a stir in the community. The mum had always been very active in school, and everyone knew her. I suppose she might have seemed neurotic to some or maybe even a touch clingy. She certainly came across as confident and happy to comment on things to do with school that she didn't agree with. I remember how cross she was when Alfie cut his hand on the branches of a bush. Even though a first aider had dealt with it, and he had recovered well, she was mortified that we had not bothered to phone her straight away. Overprotective did spring to mind when trying to describe how she behaved. She was quite controlling on the PTA even and had to have a say in every decision and every event. Yet when I think about it, she might actually seem quite timid to someone who didn't know her. Her quiet yet insistent voice, her neatly tied back hair and her fragile demeanour made her difficult to truly sum up.

I lay there, restless on the settee, and a friendly shadow emerged by the living room fireplace. Sam was tired-looking and confused. He asked if he could sit with me for a while. Beckoning him over, I made room on the settee and grabbed a pillow for him.

"I guess you know Alfie's mum died," he said, calmly.

"I had heard," I replied as he leaned towards me for a hug.

"Everyone is talking about it on WhatsApp."

"I don't think we know all the facts yet."

"Seems weird it was only this morning we had that fight. It makes me feel guilty."

"You shouldn't feel guilty at all. None of us could see this on the horizon."

"I wish we had not given him a hard time," he began to cry into my shoulder.

"Alfie hurt you both. It was one of those things. It is what it is."

"I don't know what I can do."

"Just be there for him. When he is ready, you all need to be there and support him." My arm engulfed him as he whimpered more loudly.

"Thanks, Dad. You always know what to say," he said, honestly, and with an attempt at a smile budging through endless tears.

"What on earth has happened?" Millie called as she came into the room flat-footedly.

We both looked at her with surprise and soon ushered her over to join us. We had a group hug, and Sam began to describe the unfolding news.

The fake log fire seemed to glow more than normal, and its flickers seemed to tell a story as we all sat in silence, staring at it and wondering what we could do to make the world less demanding.

The topic was a mysterious one. None of us had any clue that she was close to taking her life. We reasoned that in reality we hardly knew her at all. When we thought about it hard, it was clear she was always around and on view, but her character was a little cloudy. We just had no idea what sort of a person she really must have been. To me, she seemed regular in bringing Alfie to school and picking him up. When there was a PTA organised thing, we could guarantee she would be involved. She was never the main one running everything, and she was never particularly in our faces about it; so we truly had little to recall about her even though we must have seen her almost every day, both at work and at the post office.

I just mention the post office because Millie worked there part-time, and she had often seen an always heavily made-up Michelle in there posting parcels. Although Millie had talked about this in passing before, it all of a sudden made me want to know more.

"Well she came in twice a week, used the machine and went," said a tired Millie, scratching her head as though it might help her to recollect more facts and shed some much needed light on all of this.

"What was she like? Sheepish?" I quizzed while brewing another tea.

"Not really. She was always polite. Never needed any help."

"And yet you did not ask her where the packages were going?" I probed.

"It was not any of my actual business," she laughed. "It is not like I really cared, to be honest; but if I had wanted to know, I would not have been entitled to an answer."

"So you didn't have to take the parcel, read its address, type it into a machine or whatever?"

"No. We have a machine where the customer can weigh it and type in their details to create their own labels and then put their parcels in a box ready to send off." Millie was very formidable when she was talking about work.

"And I guess this week's parcel has already been sent off?" I tried just once more to tease out a possibility of helping to solve this problem.

"Well, I imagine so. The last time she dropped one off was yesterday, which means it would have already been sent to wherever it was going."

She confirmed my fears, sharply. I was at a dead end here, but my mind would not concede.

Sam crawled off to bed, and Millie reminded me that I had to work the next day and so should be in bed too by now. When I got in finally, I pulled the sheets over but could not let go of the idea that somehow these parcels could shed light on everything.

Chapter 10 (Alex)

How could I keep everything as normal as possible? How could I hold my head up high? Nothing made any sense to me anymore. I was overwhelmed, bewildered and out of painkillers. My head pounded slowly as it had for the past ten hours. A night spent at my mum's house was needed, but I really ought to go back there; to the home I had shared with Michelle. My heart was sat throbbing gently in the soles of my shoes. My ears quietly rang. My nose ran tirelessly. I felt as though reality had subsided, and everything was a mix between chaos and sublime fantasy. My children needed me. No doubt about that. But what could I say? What should I do? Who could I turn to? Why didn't I see any of this coming? I was not one to cry, but tears fell out of my eyes, like rain from an overloaded storm cloud suddenly offloading. Like daggers, they seemed to cut across my cheeks and dig into my jaw, carving faint yet permanent etchings across my face and staining me forever, like ageing creams; dissolving the past and dripping poignantly onto the floor, as if flooding and muddying the future and any chance of escape.

I had put a few clothes in a bag last night and got out of there as the police had urged me to. They wanted to examine the house and take finger prints and find out exactly what she did. I had accidentally taken her jumper with me. As I picked it out of the bag, I thought about the last time I had seen her in it. Just the other evening. She had been cooking salmon, and I recalled her taking it off because she said it stank of fish. I sniffed it now, and it was clean and fragrant. It reminded me of spring and the strolls we took through the hills. My heart sank back down into those soles, and I gathered myself together. My kids were stood either side of me as they saw me caress her jumper. They leant into my shoulders, and we stood in silence, looking out of the window, reflecting quietly.

I gathered up their stuff, and we got in the car quickly. My mum asked if I would be alright on the road, driving in this state. I tried to make her believe that I was capable, and I started to drive off without looking over my shoulder. I needed to face up to this. As I drove quite slowly through the mainly car-less roads, the usual warmth associated with going home did not reassemble, and I was left feeling confused, uncomfortable and out of place. I noticed a glazed look in Alfie's eyes, and the sparkle of partly evaporated tears chalked into his face. I could not determine the way Tess felt exactly, as she looked quite serious; yet I sometimes thought I could see the beginnings of a smile, especially as we passed some of our favourite haunts, like the park, the duck pond, and the place where she went to dancing lessons. I prayed to a god that I had never really believed in that she might get through this in one piece and have nothing but fond memories of her wonderful mother. Little did I know this day was going to resonate with her more strongly than anyone else. Alfie was the one with mixed emotions, so I largely anticipated him suffering greatly.

We turned into our street eventually, and I could still see the police cordon wrapped around our garden. There seemed to be no sign of anyone though, and I had been assured we could return home today. So we got out of the car slowly and were soon approached by our elderly neighbour, who hugged us all in turn and gave me some stew in a little plastic pot.

"It must be so awful for you," said Margaret as she squeezed Alfie tightly.

"We haven't really had time to get our heads around it," I replied, humbly.

"Can I stay at your house tonight?" Tess suddenly piped up, much to my astonishment.

"Of course you can, dear," said Margaret, sweetly.

Margaret had always been a great babysitter, and I was pleased that Tess was speaking but not sure if I should let her drift away so early on.

"Maybe in a few nights."

"Dad, let her go, and we can have some boy time," Alfie said, looking me in the eyes as if to say 'she needs time before she sleeps here again'.

"It will be no trouble, and we can have hot chocolate," said the old lady, warmly.

"We can make those cakes Mum and you used to make."

"Well OK. If you think that would be best."

"I just need to get used to our house without her in it," Tess said.

"Make sure you bring us some cakes too," Alfie started, winking at me discreetly.

We all stepped into the hallway, and Margaret took the kids' coats off them before we opened the living room door. Something about the place seemed overly sterile. The police had done a good job of cleaning up, but there was no clear feeling of home; just silence and coldness. I went upstairs to turn the heating on and found myself wandering into the bathroom. There was no sign of anything. No blood, not that there would have been I guess; nothing out of the norm, apart from the stark truth that my wife had killed herself in this very room.

Chapter 11 (Matt)

The weather seemed a lot more bleak the next day. I took the dog for a walk after dropping Max off at school. I had called work and taken a day off because I wanted to clear my head, and they owed me a few days, so it really made no difference anyway. I could not stop thinking about the mysterious death of Alex's wife or the horrid reality of my own sinking marriage. It was a train wreck. It had been for quite some time. After these recent events, it seemed to have come to the point where I had to really think carefully about my future, and how that future could impact on Max. In these situations, the only person I could turn to was my brother, Jamie. He would listen to me rant and not judge me, but he would also make me see sense. As I found myself edging towards his street, I suddenly had the urge to direct message the teacher again. I could not help myself. "Hi, please keep an eye on Max for me. Thanks. Matt." I left it at that, but I hoped he would at least give me an update on how the boy was doing at school. It was only yesterday that Max was in a fight on stage, and they still had another performance of their play this afternoon. His mum swore on her mother's life that she would go to this show, but I knew he was not bothered either way, as he was used to no shows when it came to her.

The wind was howling now and really blowing me about, causing the dog to get excited and my hair to break through the crust of fixing gel and start flailing around wildly. I knew I should have bought a 'super-hold' version of gel rather than the light touch one. Aesthetics went out of the window for a minute as I tried to reclaim my balance. I had lost concentration for a second and walked over a hole in the footpath, stumbling slightly and letting go of the dog lead, momentarily. The stupid dog legged it at his first chance. He was always a runner. I cannot believe I had let go so quickly. Fego was gone in an instance, and now I would spend the afternoon trying to hunt him down once more. Could this day get any better? I started to turn back for the car when a friendly face appeared in a vehicle, which had pulled up beside me. It was Nicole, my cousin, and she was eager to tell me that she had just seen what she thought was my dog racing down the high street. I hopped into her Mercedes, and we did a 360. The dog was my mission, but my head was telling me to offload a bit to Nicole while I had the opportunity. The only problem is, she would judge me. She had always seen the good in everyone. She would not make it easy for such a conversation. I decided to rein it in and chat about the suicide. A safer topic, ironically.

Nicole had to have the window open as we drove, which to me seemed crazy, as not only did it make it very cold inside that car, but it made it even harder to hold a meaningful conversation over the howling noise of the encroaching wind. Her hair swept back freely as we negotiated several bends in the street, and she had always got her radio on in the background. This meant I had to literally yell whatever I was going to say to her out loud.

She looked carefree as she drove.

"So how did Fego get away from you this time?" she shouted.

"I fell over a broken bit of kerb."

"I swear he was just around here about five minutes ago."

"He will come home eventually. He usually manages to."

"You seem like something else is puzzling you," she screamed, happily.

"Well yeah, this whole suicide thing. It doesn't make any sense. It just all of a sudden…"

"I know what you mean," she interrupted mid-sentence, "but you know she was never really happy. Their marriage was probably a sham."

"What makes you think this?" Now my curiosity was growing exponentially.

Nicole took a moment to clear her thoughts and compose herself before she replied.

"Are you kidding? She was a nervous wreck."

"How do you know? I mean I never really noticed anything unusual," I shouted back, doubtfully.

Nicole slammed on the breaks and pulled into a little lay-by. She turned off the engine and wound up the window. I could tell she was more concerned about people hearing this part, but I could see no sign of anyone around us. She moved her head closer to me and took a deep breath.

"You are not exactly the observant type, cous!" she snapped.

"What do you mean?" I replied with a defensive whine.

"You spend your whole life wrapped up in a bubble. Wrapped up in 'yourself' and 'your' world."

"How dare you! I have never done anything to cheese you off. I notice stuff!"

"But you don't! You go from place to place. You have earphones in most of the time. You unplug yourself from what is really going on at your own doorstep. I mean I am not trying to upset you but wake up and smell the coffee."

I pondered for a minute, sort of brooding over what she had asserted and wondered if I really was self-obsessed in the eyes of everyone I knew.

"I take this shit from you. I really do. I know it comes from a good place. But Nic, have a look in the mirror; will you?"

Turning the glow away from me and onto her felt refreshing for a moment before she slapped it back over to me again.

"I ain't saying I'm perfect. I mean, who is? But just friendly advice. Open your eyes a little wider. Take a look out there. Don't hide in your bubble all day."

On that note, she started the engine and drove me back to mine, where an exhausted little hound was waiting on the drive, rapidly panting. We had a cup of tea and moved onto lighter subjects. We both knew that that conversation would stay in the car and should be best left alone, for now.

Chapter 12 (Josh)

The rain was pouring down today, which meant bad news for me; as the kids would have 'wet play', and I would lose my break time looking after them while they trash the room, building Lego monstrosities and colouring in endless reams of scrap paper. Alfie was not at school today, understandably, and his sister was also off. The children were drawn to conversations which suggested some kind of paranormal mystery attached to Michelle's untimely death. I did not have the energy to challenge them each time. As I sat at my desk, devouring a Mars bar, I heard two boys excitedly going at it back and forth, suggesting a story worthy of Spielberg.

"Aliens came during the day…but not like ordinary aliens; these ones were clever," James said, candidly.

"Yeah they dressed up as post men (sniggering slightly) and used their disguises to access her house," continued Kieran, smiling.

"Clever aliens?" I found myself unable to keep out of it.

"Sorry, sir," they chanted, awkwardly.

"No, come on. Tell me about your conspiracy theory. I am interested."

James piped up, "It's just what people are saying online. You know…"

"We hear about this stuff all of the time," Kieran added in a matter-of-fact kind of way.

"I think it is a shame that when something awful happens like this, everyone is gossiping about it. You should be showing that you care for your friend, Alfie. He is having a very rough time," I barked, sternly.

The two boys got back to their sketching, and I took myself out of the room to ask a passing teaching assistant to grab me a coffee. She smiled and soon returned with a warm container of my favourite blend. I could tell that she was worried about me as her eyes frowned sympathetically. Maybe I came across as feeling sorry for myself.

Scanning my Facebook later, I saw a post from Matt. It said that he had spent the morning on a wild goose chase, trying to find his runaway dog. The way he wrote was funny and brought a smile to my mouth as I scooped up the lukewarm Bolognese that I scrounged from the dinner ladies. The staff room was bustling, and it felt as though everyone was talking about Michelle. The head came over to me to see how I was.

"Have you had a chat with the class yet?" she said, sweetly.

"Not yet, not as such, although they are all talking about it," I replied, calmly.

"Do you want me there when you do it? I am sorry I was not in this morning, as I was on a course."

"It would be good to have you there, as I just do not know how to deal with their questions," I said, with genuine relief.

We had that awkward conversation later on, as the class sat dumbstruck in contemplation. A few sobbed gently as the head added to my comments and encouraged them to go and speak to the school counsellor if they needed to talk it through. She was always good with things like this. It came so easily to her. I was not too bad but had a lot to learn from her. Nobody chose to ask any questions, but Mark put his hand up to say something.

"I just wanted to say that we all are really shocked by this and whatever the reasons for it…we all need to be there to support Alfie and Tess," he said, emotionally.

It was unusual for him to pipe up about anything, so I felt particularly impressed at his braveness. The other kids nodded their heads in agreement, and then the bell went to tell them to go home. As I was clearing up the room, Mrs Bellamy, or

Sue as we called her when the kids weren't around, hung about to have another chat with me.

"There will be a funeral soon, and I am wondering whether we should close the class for the day, as so many of them will probably want to be there," she said, sombrely.

I thought for a moment and realised that this meant I would be expected to go. I had not really had time to think about this, but it came to mind that Matt would be there and that made me feel a mixture of happy and uncomfortable. Seeing him again would be nice, but not at a funeral where I had to console my son. At a time where he would be surrounded by his own family? Well, I soon realised that it would be very busy, and there would be no need for awkwardness, as we were all going to be there for the same reason…to pay our respects to Michelle.

Chapter 13 (Alex)

Waking up to find Alfie showering in my en-suite, I considered for a minute using the family bathroom, but it still was too soon to spend time in there. Even though I had never seen any blood because the police did such a good job of cleaning up, it was going to remain a place that I stayed clear of. Both of the kids used my shower instead of going in there. None of us could handle what had happened, and that room had become some kind of shrine to her. Michelle had died in that bath; and today, we were going to have to deal with the reality of it. Today was going to be her funeral.

My mum and dad came around very early and were quickly chasing the kids to get ready and making a hearty fried breakfast to help us prepare for what was going to be the most challenging day since the passing. I had a speech in my head and some notes to help me remember key points. Composing myself I ran through it while looking into a mirror. I wanted to make sure I was smart for her, meaning I wore my best suit and slicked my hair so as to be as presentable as I could manage. The kids looked handsome, and both seemed to be holding it together well, at least until we saw that car draw up next to our driveway.

I drew strength from my kids normally, but right now I felt alone. I genuinely did not know how to be a parent without Michelle. Part of me thought she was selfish for doing this. It made no sense; and I half-wondered if people would think it was down to me. Was I a bad husband not to realise that she was upset? Would people jeer me when we arrived at the funeral? Were people around here ever going to be able to look at me in the same way again? I had no answers right now, but what I did know was that all of us were going to sit in a slow-moving vehicle, following a coffin, as she made her final journey to her resting place.

Our marriage wasn't perfect. I know she loved me. She should have known that I loved her back. We argued once in a while about not clearing up the kitchen or forgetting to feed the cat, but aside from that we got on just fine. I genuinely felt like I had lost my best friend; and that, there was no returning from what had happened. Our lives had been changed for good. But there was nothing 'good' about it. As we sat there, next to each other, all trying hard not to cry, Alfie nudged me and asked, "What happens to Mum now? Will she just rot away under the ground?"

This set me off, and tears suddenly drained from my eye sockets as I clutched him close and said, "She will be alright, mate. She will be looked after. Just remember that she loved you guys more than anything, and today we are here to celebrate the life she led. You are her superstars."

Tess leaned over and gave me a kiss on the cheek, and we returned to silence, watching the misty English countryside roll by. It wouldn't be long before they were all staring at us, casting their eyes upon us with suspicion and fake pity. Well, maybe not everyone. If I was going to think like that, then I would never be able to live here happily again. I told myself that positivity was the only way forward, as I had a lot of responsibility on my shoulders now; and the kids deserved a caring dad who was always there for them, not a blithering wreck like I was becoming.

Arriving in the car park, the beautiful church stood over us hauntingly, reminding me of the wedding and christenings that we had shared there. Time had flown by since those, and now everyone was looking much more serious. Mourning was a difficult beast, and one that didn't sit well with me. But it was coming face to face with people who could not contain their grief that wound me up. Some of the people in the crowd awaiting our arrival were sobbing dramatically. Typically, it was mostly the people who hardly knew her or spent very little time with her; the pompous ladies of the Parent Teacher Association, the neighbours who normally never even spoke as we went about our daily routines, and the awkward strangers who I could not identify as recognisable figures from Michelle's past.

Chapter 14 (Josh)

When we got there, the funeral car was already driving into the car park, and I could see a waiting crowd just outside the door of this historic church. Only slightly delayed after picking up Mrs Bellamy from town, we straightened ourselves out, and Sam clutched firmly to my hand as we made our way over to the entrance. We could see Matt sat with his wife and son about halfway down the packed-out hall. Mrs Bellamy had to be close to the front because she was giving a speech. She had asked us to come with her, as they had apparently saved us some seats. It was uncomfortable to see Alex stood right in front of me, chatting to the vicar, probably finalising the running order. He looked calm but shattered, pretty much a fragment of his former self.

Sam was directly behind Alfie; and when they spotted each other, Alfie extended his hand and shook it, thanking him for coming. It was good to see that they had no hard feelings after the assembly debacle. Usually with boys, any tiffs were soon forgotten; and in this case, the situation seemed to bring them closer together. I knew that Sam had been keeping in touch with both Alfie and Max on a daily basis.

Before long, the tension increased, and the voices lowered. A sad organ sound emitted music that was heart-wrenching and immediately brought tears to my eyes. Sam lowered his head in grief, and I could see him touch Alfie on the shoulder tenderly to remind him that he was there for him. My heart broke as I saw Alex return carrying the coffin, with Michelle's brother the other side, and her father following on at the back. What a horrible thing for anyone to have to deal with, burying his own flesh and blood. Glancing over my shoulder, I could tell that Max wasn't handling it very well, and he was being comforted by a very sombre-looking Matt, shaved of all of his usual hotness, dissolved into a humble guy, respectfully commemorating the life of a family friend. I felt even more admiration for him at this most inappropriate of moments. I turned back and gave Sam a close hug, and then we started to sing the first hymn.

I could hear Max crying now quite loudly, even as Alfie stayed calm and seemed to be internalising his pain. Footsteps told me that Max had run off, and Sam flew past me to go and find him. Following on, I was soon stood in a windy graveyard with my boy leaning over his friend, trying to console him. Behind me, a voice reached out to me. We were enough of a distance away from the boys so as not to be heard.

"It's wrong, isn't it. This should not be happening," Matt said.

I looked at him and sighed. "They will get through this, and it will make men of them," I said, reluctantly.

"I have been thinking," he carried on almost as if he were talking on the breeze, hiding his words, "I enjoyed hanging out with you, man."

I was taken aback as the conversation redirected suddenly.

"I mean we should probably do it again some time," he said, with a very honest smile, made slightly odd as it was underwritten by tears.

With the boys still talking through everything, I decided to take this forward.

"I like you. OK. You may not want to deal with this, but I think we get on really well. We have something," I gulped as I tried to undo what I had just said. "You know, we can be great mates."

Not sure that I had covered my tracks, he smiled again.

"We do have something, and I want to explore that with you," he winked, cheekily.

This was the most peculiar thing. Here we were, dealing with a friend's wife being buried, and he was undeniably flirting with me. My heart did not know how to respond. I felt it stop for a moment, but then it swiftly raced and fluttered again.

"That would be definitely worthwhile."

My reply was confident and unexpected. What had come over me?

Sam shouted for us to go back in as he gathered Max up and drew him over to the church door. Now was not the time to be considering having an affair with my son's friend's dad.

Time passed, and the coffin was brought outside where a few closing speeches included one from Alex, who stood over the grave, shivering and intense.

"I remember when we met..." he began, sweetly. I thought that, out of the corner of my eye, I spotted Hannah make a strange gesture, as if to mimic a small vomiting movement like when you pretend to 'reach' after somebody tells you something cheesy. It couldn't have been the case as when I looked again she was stood motionless and without expression, standing erect, next to a much taller Matt. I knew how much he had grown to resent her, and this made me feel less guilty about considering the idea of having an affair.

The speech was very moving, and again we were all in tears. We collected our things from the church, and most people went on to the scout hall for the wake. Sam had said that he didn't feel comfortable going to that, as he thought it would mainly be for family, and I could see that the whole thing had exhausted him. My boss also did not want to stay for this part and so was happy for me to give her a lift and use that as an excuse for going home instead of facing the possibility of parents coming up to us and asking unrelated questions about school. Wherever we went, they would find ways to turn conversations towards how they could improve their child's progress, or what we could do to promote their child, perhaps handing out responsibilities or moving their lockers so that they weren't next to 'such and such'.

I dropped off Mrs Bellamy and while Sam sat drooped, half-asleep on the back seat, I contemplated the future. How would Alex now cope as a single parent? Did it mean that Alfie would go off the rails? Was Matt really going to 'explore' our relationship? One thing was for sure, the next few months and years were going to be very interesting indeed. Little did I know how much impact the last couple of weeks' events were going to have on our futures.

Part Two – The Sons
Ten Years Later

Chapter 15 (Sam)

It was always interesting having your dad as a teacher, but having your dad as a gay teacher could end up with you getting teased a bit about the whole thing. I didn't mind though. I could handle it because I liked the fact that my dad had been brave enough to come out and show his true self. The only problem was, him seeing one of my friend's parents. This is one thing that I just could not get my head around, and it all happened so fast.

Even though that was a week ago and so much had happened since, I still found myself reliving the moment when I discovered them together. If my guitar lesson hadn't been cancelled, then I would have still been none the wiser; and Dad could have carried on with his sordid little affair without all of this backlash.

"Hey queer's boy!" came a predictable shout from John across the football pitch. "Pass the ball, faggot."

I turned around and looked for a better way forward. Noticing Alfie running alongside me, I tossed the ball to him, and the pressure was then off. Alfie surged forward; and as he passed John, he elbowed him in the face. John jolted and then clutched his chin whilst looking at me with disapproval. I shrugged my shoulders as if to say, 'It wasn't anything to do with me'.

Later on in the changing rooms, Alfie made a snide comment.

"You think it's alright to be homophobic on the pitch, do you? Professionals get kicked out for doing anything like that, you know," he said to John, pointedly.

John was afraid of Alfie and just looked the other way, packing his bag as quickly as he could so that he could escape sheepishly.

"Don't waste your breath," I said to Alfie. "It's no skin off my nose."

He tutted and then said he would buy me a coke if I wanted. He wasn't that keen to go home just yet.

In the coffee shop, we sat down in silence, and it was obvious that his mind was elsewhere. It would have been ten years next week since his mother died. All of my problems seemed miniature in comparison. I thought about what I could say to cheer him up, but sadly, nothing appropriate crossed my uncomplicated mind.

We sipped our drinks and stared out of the window for a while. After a few minutes, I asked him how he was coping.

"I'm alright, mate," he replied, faking a smile.

"You don't have to hide your feelings from me. We have been through a lot over the last ten years."

"I know. It's just this time it is different. I mean it's not so much about my mum anymore."

"How do you mean?" I asked as I finished off the coke.

"It's just I can't really put my finger on it, but it's kind of about Tess," he carried on, getting into his stride.

"Go on…what about your little sis?" I asked, getting more and more worried. "Is it that guy she is seeing? I thought he was a bit of a creep. If he has done anything to her, I will smash his face in for you," I said, tensing a fist and raising it in the air.

He knew I always had a protective streak when it came to Tess.

"If only it were that simple. I'd have knocked his block off ages ago if that were all it was," he retorted, almost laughing.

"Well if there is anything I can do to help then just say, mate," I went on.

"I will let you know."

He looked at me with eyes that told me to leave it alone for a bit, and we both grabbed our stuff. Just as I was about to sit on my saddle, he stopped me with his hand.

"What do you know about depression?" he said in a matter-of-fact kind of way.

I was honest and shook my head in order to show him that I knew very little on this matter.

"Never mind then," he carried on, waving me off.

"But I can find out about it," I shouted as I cycled off into the distance.

He yelled back at me. "Talk to Tess. See whether you think she is depressed. She will open up to you."

When I got home, the first thing I decided to do was to text Tess. I wasn't quite sure what to put as I hadn't seen her for a while. I kept it simple with a "Hi Tess, how have you been lately? Did you hear the new Shawn Mendes song?" I knew that she loved him; and lately, I had been getting his new track stuck in my head, especially as my dad always played it in the car.

Grabbing a shower and flicking through YouTube for a bit, it took me a while to realise that she had texted me back. Her reply was short and to the point. "Hi. Fine. No."

It wasn't the type of text you came to expect from Tess, as she usually liked to fill your screen with long, rambling sentences and smiley emoticons. I replied to ask if she wanted to talk about it? She simply sent me an ellipsis (…).

I was suddenly really worried now. Something was definitely not right.

Chapter 16 (Max)

My stutter was becoming less of a burden these days. I decided that I should face my fears and join a drama group. After everything blowing up with my dad, I needed somewhere to outlet my feelings. Disguising myself as someone else, cloaked in their character and mindset, might just do the trick. The sixth form play was coming up, and I was not prepared for it to go as badly as that dreaded one ten years before. The day when I ended up hurt, and Alfie's mum killed herself.

I wanted to find a way to overcome my nerves. Maybe this was going to do the trick. Alfie lit the roll up and took a few deep sucks to get it started. The spliff was fairly smoky to begin with but soon settled down, and he passed it to me. After a bit of getting used to it and coughing a few times, I handed it back again.

"That should get you ready for your audition," he said as he took another puff; his eyes flickering, and his face looking flushed. We sat there for a while, throwing stones into the river and chilling out in the afternoon sun.

"I'd better go, or I will be late. Wish me luck."

"You can do it, dimwit," he said, affectionately.

Being the only one to drive, I hopped into my mini and made my way to the drama theatre at school. It was a six o'clock audition, so the car park was empty. School had long since closed, and the place looked like a ghost town. Running towards the theatre door, my friend Lisa joined me, and we signed our names on a sheet before entering the main room. Mr Simmons looked at us both and smiled. He was always good at putting anyone at ease, but the spliff was even better.

It had definitely made me feel as though I were floating. Lisa could tell I had been up to something.

"You stink!" She had moaned when we first met up.

While we waited for our turns, I borrowed some of her perfume to douse the smell of the weed. She told me that it did the trick but laughed because I now smelt like a teenage girl. That was the least of my worries. The teacher called my name, and I made my way slowly and nervously to the centre of that darkened stage.

Lisa gave me the thumbs up, and I went through those lines that I had been rehearsing for the past week. My character was meant to be angry; and, right now, I felt like I could portray angry quite well. I tensed my fist and shrugged a lot as I bellowed my 12 lines towards the director. The few people who were watching nearby gave me a small applause, and I sat back down next to Lisa before watching her stand and walk over to the same spot to try out her segment. She laughed as she got muddled over one of the lines. Despite this, she still seemed to pull it off well. It would have been great if we both got a role and could go through the script together. She was so much fun to be around after all. A chance to spend more time with her alone would be well received as far as I was concerned.

I went home to find Mum going through some of Dad's things. She looked fed up, and I asked her if she wanted a cup of tea or something, but she just shook her head and carried on sorting stuff into piles. When I came back from making myself a drink, she was outside starting a fire. I could see a pile of clothes slowly starting to burn. Running out to stop her, she pushed me away and began to cry. She hurried indoors, and I used the hose pipe to put out the fire, but the clothes were already ruined. When I returned inside, Mum was sitting on the kitchen floor, sobbing and rocking slowly. I tried to give her a hug; and this time, for once, she allowed me to. We sat there for about half an hour before I was able to convince her to go to bed and rest. She never said a word but forced a smile as I guided her towards the staircase. I was straight on the phone to Sam, wondering if he had seen my elusive father.

Sam picked up and I had it out with him. People used to think that I was weedy and shy, but when I got riled up about something, I just let rip! Sam's ears were probably bleeding as he quietly listened, saying 'mhmm' once in a while to suggest that he was still with me. After I had gone on about how his dad had destroyed my mum's marriage, I calmed down a bit, and we had a more ordinary conversation. To be honest, it was hard to stay mad at Sam, as he was a genuinely nice guy. It wasn't his fault at all. Calming me down further, Sam offered to meet up and talk more, but he also told me that Alfie was beginning to worry about Tess. I wondered why he never mentioned it earlier on when we were smoking by the park. Sam just sort of dropped it into the conversation, perhaps to distract me further. Both Sam and I had always looked out for Tess. We worried that one day her mum's death might get to her. Maybe that time had finally come. It was bound to at some point, and we didn't think Alfie would be much use in those circumstances. I grabbed my coat and popped to see Sam and find out what he had managed to discover so far.

Chapter 17 (Alfie)

Dad was struggling more than ever. He needed me to pull my weight around the house. We needed to help each other out. When I got home, he was scratching his head and looking through a pile of what looked like paper bills. Dad being Dad, he was never that good at talking about his problems. He would always just plod along and try and cover everything up, pretending that there was no issue to worry about. He had been like this his whole life, but especially since Mum passed away.

"Do you want me to get a part-time job? Probably about time I did something," I said as I entered the living room.

"No. I promised you that I would support you through your A-Levels, and I will. You will have enough on your plate when you get to university," he replied, sweetly.

I looked at him with serious eyes.

"I can see that you are struggling, Dad. Most boys my age have jobs of some kind. I am on top of my school work. I could do every Sunday at Waitrose and earn double time."

He came over to me and gave me a fatherly hug.

"We do have a few more bills than usual at the moment. The washing machine breaking down didn't help things, but now we have that trouble with the boiler. I shall have to ask your nan for help. But that's my problem. Not yours."

I heard what he was saying, but a few minutes later, I headed to my room with my iPad in hope of finding an application form, so that I could get a Sunday job as soon as possible.

My sister's door was closed, with a sign hanging from it saying, in bold letters, 'Chill Time'; and a picture of a rabbit sitting, eating a carrot while basking in the sun. Loud rock music was almost rattling the door off, and so I found myself banging on it to get her to turn it down a bit.

"Go away!" she yelled with a tone that told me she was in no mood to negotiate.

I stormed in anyway, finding her laying on her bed, browsing through some unknown items. To me it looked like a pirate had just been discovered counting their treasures. She gathered them away and then stuck two fingers up at me. Younger sisters were meant to be difficult, but lately, she seemed to have more angst than I had ever seen.

"What is your problem?" I announced.

"Screw you!" came her curt reply.

"What is that you are keeping in that bloody box?" I went on.

"None of your bloody business, knob head," she continued with an expression that implied she was hiding something.

"I dunno why you are so cross with me. I ain't done anything," I moaned.

"I just have a lot on my mind."

"But don't take it out on us. Dad is really struggling at the moment."

"Dad just gets on with it. Sometimes he needs to get a grip of things. Maybe if he did, Mum would still be around."

I had never heard her talk like that before. Especially about Dad. Alarmingly, she even dared to mention Mum. She hadn't uttered her name for as long as I could remember. She usually did everything in her power to avoid conversations linked to our mum.

I was speechless, so I decided to leave her to it. Wondering what she was going on about, I sat with my headphones on and quickly started searching for job application forms. It didn't sit easily with me that she had slagged Dad off, but I was not prepared to argue with her. Maybe she was just lashing out because she was on her period. Typical girl.

As I sat browsing through websites, a message flashed up from her on my messenger. It simply said, "Sorry, bro."

A tear formed in my eye when I read it. I just wished I could help her. I typed back, "I forgive you, midget," using her nickname; one that Mum used to use because she was very small as a toddler. Nowadays though, she was as tall as me, so the nickname was ironic.

Finding a job that I liked, I carried on form filling. She turned down her music; and Dad could be heard on the phone, talking to his mother, probably asking her for a loan. Sam texted me to say he was meeting up with Max, but I felt too tired to go out again. I switched on the computer and loaded up my favourite shoot-em-up. I was going to use some of that gathered up energy to blast some invading droids.

Chapter 18 (Sam)

After convincing Tess to meet me in the milkshake hut, a few days later, I was glad to see her arrive, dressed with an edge, reflecting her feisty character. Maybe Tess was back to her old self. I was getting her one of her favourites, a mix of strawberries and banana, topped with marshmallow bits, when she rolled in and sat on the table where I had left my bag. Nodding at me in order to show that she knew I was here, she then proceeded to get her iPad out and start tapping away. Her fingers typed quickly as she sat in the plastic seat, with her eyes focussed on the screen intently. This was not so much the girl that I used to know. She seemed to be on a mission.

"I'm writing a book," she snapped before I had chance to even greet her with a 'hi'.

I was a bit taken aback, but, placing her drink next to her and putting my own milkshake down, I wanted to probe her a bit about this so-called book.

"Cool. I had no idea you wanted to be a writer," I said, celebrating the choice.

"I am no author, but I do have a story to tell," she barked, not in a nasty way but in a sort of 'screw you world!' way. She forced a smile for a moment and said some more.

"I have always liked you. That is why I don't mind telling you a bit about my book. It is based on real life, so that makes it kind of sensitive."

Wondering whether I was going to feature in this book, I asked her for more detail.

"I can't tell you everything as I am still researching. However, I can say it is all about putting one massive wrong right," she replied, now more quietly, checking over her shoulder for anyone who might be listening.

I found myself also looking over my shoulder each time that I said something. Expecting her to find the whole thing amusing, I waited to see what came next.

"My mum died nearly ten years ago, give or take," she said, in a curious whisper. "She died because of someone else. It wasn't as straight forward as everyone thinks. She had been suffering for a long time, and now I am going to get retribution for her."

"But where did this idea come from? You have never spoken about her like this. What brought that on?" I asked as I worried about her state of mind.

"If you aren't going to listen and take this seriously, then you're not the man I thought you were," she growled, snapping her iPad cover down and turning to look me in the eye.

"Mum was being bullied. I know that for sure. I just am not a 100% certain why. But I do think I know who."

I took a big gulp of milkshake and contemplated calling for back-up, as I was starting to realise that she really was in a weird state.

Where did she get all of this from? Why did she suddenly have these feelings?

I pressed her further on it. Tess was typing away the whole time that I spent discussing it with her. She didn't seem to want to give me any details or even any clues as to why she was so intent on exposing whatever this turned out to be.

"You must have seen or heard something that made you think this," I said. "You didn't always reckon it was anyone's fault. The police were alarmed by the scene and checked it over; didn't they? They ruled out everything that night, and the coroner said it was definitely suicide."

She looked up from her writing and scowled at me.

"I don't like talking about it as suicide. Mum wasn't that selfish. She was upset. She was harassed. She was at the end of her tether, and she could see no other way out," she replied, angrily.

I was offended that she felt I was being disrespectful, wondering how we could ever discuss this issue properly if every word spoken had to be on her terms. I decided to go for the safest option and just listen to whatever Tess wanted to say. She sipped her drink and leaned forward.

"I haven't told Dad or Alfie about any of this, but Alfie nearly discovered my secret box the other day."

I was obviously puzzled, but she soon cleared this up a bit.

"Mum had left me a box around my neighbour's house. She had instructed Margaret to give it to me when I turned 16. Well…dumbo…I just turned 16, and she handed it over to me. She told me that Mum had given it to her about a week before she passed away. When I asked Margaret why she never mentioned this, she told me she had been sworn to secrecy; and she had no idea of my mum's intentions, so she decided to honour it. I knew she hadn't looked inside as the Sellotape was still tightly wrapping the red little box."

"Wow!" I gasped, drinking my milkshake right up. "I can't believe she did that."

"Well, it makes sense to me. Margaret was a brilliant friend to both of us, and she is a very loyal lady. I don't have any bad feelings at all. But it has opened my eyes," she went on.

Her phone screen flashed, and she urgently packed up her things and started off before telling me that she was late to her piano lesson. I waved and smiled warmly, but she didn't stop long enough to make an expression before she ran out of the door.

All of these revelations didn't sit well with me. I was not sure now what to do, but I hoped that she might trust me enough to show me some of the contents of this mysterious gift. Perhaps I could get Alfie to have a sneaky hunt for it, and we could examine it ourselves. I thought better of it and decided the best person to speak to about all of this was Max, as he had his head screwed on and usually knew the best way to deal with these things. After a chat on messenger, he vowed to help me sort this out.

Chapter 19 (Max)

It was our first read through together, and the air outside was warm and wet. Lisa was so excitable, as she had not thought she would get any role at all; but she successfully got the female lead, and I got a major role too, it turned out. Sadly, I wasn't her love interest, but I did have lots of lines to learn; and my character was meant to hang around the stage for eight scenes, which meant I had to find a way to handle those lifelong, crippling nerves of mine. One thing was certain; having Lisa there was going to make it much more bearable.

Today we all sat around a table, going through every line and discussing possible staging. The director, Mr Simmons, was very helpful and guided us kindly through each scene, suggesting ways we could alter our tone and bring out the characters appropriately. He was a legend in school, and we all took what he said very seriously, often taking time to note down his suggestions. My scripts ended up covered in copious notes, which I would probably have to type up later in order to make sense of them. The reviews for last year's play were outstanding, and none of us wanted to let the others down. We all badly wanted to pull off a masterpiece, and the concentration on our faces must have looked intense.

My phone vibrated, and I caught it in time to send it to voicemail, but everyone seemed to glare at me as I tried to play it down. Dad then texted me, and I could see that it flashed up with the words 'pizza later?' This brought out a smile, which distracted me from what I was about to say.

"Keep up, Max," Mr Simmons nudged, supportively.

Lisa repeated her cue to me, and I managed to get through a few sentences correctly, even pausing for effect whilst showing a concerned expression on my face. A small clap came about as I completed the monologue, and a few more people read their lines before we were stopped and told to get a drink or use the washrooms.

Taking the opportunity to message Dad back, I agreed a time, and he said he would pick me up. It was great because I hadn't seen him for over a week now. I wondered if he had been around Sam's house, but he hadn't mentioned it, and I hadn't bothered to ask. With Sam and me, the less said about our two dads at the moment, the better. Since we both discovered them together, we had been a bit emotionally scarred. I mean, I love gay people. I love my dad. I always thought Sam's dad was great. But putting all of those elements together at the same time freaked me out. It would just take some getting used to I supposed, and the last thing I wanted was for it to drive a wedge between Dad and me. It was partly my fault though that Mum found out; as in my distress, I had messaged Chloe for support, and she had told her nan, who just happened to be my neighbour, old Ruby. So taken aback, Ruby had gone straight around to tell my very surprised mum, who immediately flipped out, threw a toaster across the room, nearly hitting me and chucked everything that Dad possessed into bin bags, dumping them in the driveway.

Anyway, that was over with; the dust was settling, and it was important that Dad and I got to spend some quality time together. When he came to pick me up after rehearsals, he nodded at me to get in the car and drove off quickly, hardly speaking all the way there. When we sat down in Pizza Bob's, I made the first move and asked him what he had been up to. He was friendly and relieved that I was still speaking to him. I was, of course, likewise pleased that he was not holding a grudge. We managed to make some small talk, and he mentioned how bad the football game had been the previous night, and how our favourite team's manager was appalling and should have been sacked. We definitely agreed on that. It made him laugh when I did an impression of the ignorant goalie who was basically not even paying attention when the striker came by and scored from up close. Dad seemed at ease with me, so I considered bringing up Josh, my old teacher.

"Where are you living, Dad?" I asked.

"Just with my cousin, Nicole. Thought you knew," he replied, calmly.

"I don't have much to do with her because I don't have her number. So I just assumed you had your own place or were living with Josh," I said, awkwardly.

He shook his head and tutted. I could tell that he did not know what to say.

"Look mate, I never wanted it to be this way. I tried so hard with your mum for so long, but she just blocked me out every time. She never gave me the time of day. I don't want to sound mean, but she was always preoccupied and never showed any interest in my life."

I couldn't handle this, even though I was sure that he was correct. Many times I had seen her blank him or just shrug him off. She basically treated him like shit, but I turned a blind eye every time, assuming that was normal for two parents. After all, they loved each other. That was what I had thought, but now everything seemed based on lies. Thinking about bringing up the obvious, my mind was changed by an interruption that I could not have foreseen.

Alex came through the door to the restaurant and paced over to the counter, looking as if he were expecting to pick up a take away. He clocked us straight away and nodded to Dad, with a smile. Dad got up and went over to him, and they chatted quietly for a while before they both came over and spoke to me.

"Thanks for always looking out for Alfie," said Alex as he patted my shoulder supportively. "You know you are welcome around ours any time."

"We all get on well. We just look out for each other," I replied, quietly.

"I worry that he smokes too much weed," he went on.

Dad looked at me with a grimace, indicating we might need to discuss this further afterwards.

"He doesn't do much, I promise. He is fairly chilled and looks after himself. I think he worries about Tess though."

This change of subject was my way of getting off that awkward topic. I knew that Alfie was smoking spliffs like it was going out of fashion and didn't want Dad grilling me about it.

"What makes you think that?"

Alex was surprised that I had snuck that into the conversation randomly.

"I dunno, guess he is just being an overprotective big brother," I said, trying hard to dig my way out of another awkward topic.

"Do you think he has a reason to worry about something?" pressed my dad, throwing his hat into the ring.

My head was spinning. This really was not the direction I wanted to go in.

"Whatever it is, I will get to the bottom of it, but both of you please just let us sort it. If you go prying, Tess will freak out."

Well and truly feeling told off, both men chuckled, and Alex was called over to pay for his pizzas. He waved as he left and nearly fell over as the door opened in his face. Relentless as the night was, coming into the place now was a rather drenched-looking Lisa.

She was telling Alex to pull up his hood, when she too noticed us sat by the window.

"Hey!" She yelled, still dripping like a wet sponge, with her hair glued to her forehead.

Dad invited her to join us and looked impressed that a reasonably hot girl was interested in hanging out with me.

"Are you taking out or do you want to join us?" he asked.

Being polite she made her excuses, but I tried to reinforce the offer, as I could sense that she didn't really fancy going back out into the rain.

"Dude, you are gonna get soaked. Just stay here and dry off with us. We can discuss the play."

Quickly she agreed, and soon we were all happily talking about rehearsals. Dad was quizzing us on the process of learning our lines, and we were bitching about some of the other actors and their diva demands.

"Jake said he couldn't rehearse well without a constant supply of coconut juice, and Cara insisted that she stopped every half hour for a cup of green tea," Lisa said, rolling her eyes disapprovingly.

The pizza was colourful, with a healthy mix of vegetables and meat. We were all feeling stuffed by the time it came to pay the bill. Lisa insisted on paying, but Dad ignored her and forked out for the meal before offering her a lift home, which she rejected, as she had her bike parked nearby. All seemed good with the world, but I realised when I got home that Lisa being there had stopped me having a heart to heart with Dad about Josh and him. At the same time, me leaking the fact that Tess was having problems may have let the cat out of the bag and started a whole load of new issues. As I lay in bed, waiting to fall asleep, I thought about going to see Tess the next morning and getting to the bottom of everything before somebody else got in there first; that somebody being the last person in the world she wanted to know. Her dad.

Failing to drift off to sleep, I ran my lines for the play through my head a few times and was oblivious for a while of the fact that a text message had landed on my iPad screen. It was from Lisa.

"Had a great time tonight. Even if your dad is a bit mixed up right now, he is still brilliant! You're so lucky to have him. Hope we hang out more. Lisa."

Blimey! I did not see that coming. It reminded me that her dad had run away many years ago with the woman that used to child-mind her when she was little. Thinking of how to respond, I was overwhelmed by a sense of achievement. Who'd have thought that a random pizza night with Dad would have led to Lisa showing some actual interest in me? I slept on that idea and hoped to dream about where that might lead to in future.

Chapter 20 (Sam)

It was freezing outside, but we were supposed to be playing football. The PE teacher was distracted somewhere, and the three of us just wanted to go in. Alfie was shivering because the wind was so icy cold. I was rubbing my hands together frantically, desperate to get through this as quickly as possible. Max, however, was too busy talking to notice the sub-zero temperatures forcing his hairs to stand on ends.

"So I went around to see your sister this morning, but she had already gone. You must have been doing your paper round," he said to Alfie.

"Yes. She normally goes out early. You know what she is like. Always doing something. Usually something strange."

"It's funny you say that," I said, interrupting them. "Because I saw her walking out of your street at about 8:30, looking peed off."

"Isn't that where her mate lives. You know...what's her name? Sally?" he replied, pacing up and down, with his hair flapping madly.

"No. She is at the other side of the village," corrected Max, without hesitation.

"That's a bit weird then, mate," said Alfie, looking perplexed. "You ask her about it, Sam."

"Don't worry, I will."

The game continued when the coach returned, and later on we all went our separate ways. My first job was to catch Tess before she left school. I reckoned she would most likely be in the ICT suite as she liked to geek out at school, and apart from everything else, she was still the school's blog editor. True enough, there she was, concentrating hard on a screen that was filled with text and pressing buttons repeatedly in a way that implied she was getting cross.

"Hey, you. What's new?" I joked as I swung past her and plonked myself on the chair next to the neighbouring computer.

"Getting sick of predictive text," she moaned, sulkily.

"Let me cheer you up," I said, revealing a snapchat picture on my phone which showed Andy from class ten being caught with his pants down, having had a wee in the bushes behind the bike sheds.

"Maybe that should go in the blog," she teased, snatching my phone from me. "Hasn't he heard of toilets?"

"To be fair, they are always out of action. This place is falling apart, and you know it," I replied, obstinately.

Having now got her attention, I asked her if she had got anywhere with her investigation. To my surprise, she came right out and told me where she had been for the past few mornings.

"I have been spying on someone. A person that I think gave my mum a lot of grief. I want to know if this person is as bad as Mum made out."

My mind was so blown away by her openness that I just had no idea how to come back from this.

"You have spied on someone? What the…?" It was my guarded response.

"Yes. Mum was clear that this woman had given her grief for many years. She was bullied by her. So much so that it reduced my mother to a blithering wreck!"

Her face screwed up with such disgust as she spoke about it. I wondered if she would tell me how she knew.

"Who is this woman? How do you know about all this?"

"My box of stuff. I told you. Mum left a diary in there. It's all in that book. Everything. It's horrible to read," she carried on, welling up and shaking a little.

I threw an arm around her and rocked her a little.

"What else was in the box?" I asked, patiently.

"My nan's engagement ring. She wanted me to have it, so she put it in there too," she said, through sniffles and occasional gasps.

"I don't know what to say."

"Don't say anything then. Just listen," she snapped.

"Do you want to do this here?" I checked, sensitively.

"Why not? Nobody is around. Here is as good as anywhere."

Tess went on to tell me how she had been finding it difficult to sleep at night ever since she found out. She believed whole-heartedly that this other woman had ruined her mum's life and led to her death. Reminding me of the fact that she had slit her wrists in the bath, Tess spoke about how lifeless her mum had felt. She apparently described in her diary the constant bitchy comments and horrid behaviour towards her. This woman had gone out of her way to make her feel useless, worthless and not worthy of being a mum or of deserving a happy life. None of the details were explicit, but I was becoming certain that Tess had some good evidence for what she was saying. To make it even clearer, she produced a small jotting book from the depths of the school bag.

"Here it is," she said, passing me the book which had got yellow post-it notes attached to some of the pages.

I looked at her with inquisitive eyes. Did she really want me to read it?

"Have a look at where I put the first post-it," she said, nudging me.

Opening that page, I saw some hand written notes which were neat and tidy and used the most exquisite handwriting I had ever seen. I began to read:

"Today was hell…again! She intercepted me while we were waiting for the kids. Standing behind me, she spoke quietly into my ear. She called me a 'bitch' and snarled that I should go away somewhere, run off and make a new life. She told me she would look after my family, and they wouldn't miss me, as I was a piece of dirt that nobody wanted to know. Everyone would be better off without me."

She had underlined 'better off without me' three times.

"This is so bad!" I said, feeling stuck between a rock and a hard place. On one hand I wanted to continue to be her confidante, and on the other, I wanted to go and tell Alfie and Alex straight away.

"You can't tell anyone," she said, with a serious face. "If you do, I don't know what I'll do. Mum trusted me with this. I need to deal with it somehow."

She trembled as she spoke. Her words were clear but somehow resonated in a darker way than usual. All of this made me feel like she was in a very bad place. I knew that I couldn't risk knocking her over the edge. She really was capable of anything.

"And I don't want to see Max," she said, as we both got up, ready to go.

"What do you mean?" I asked, with concern.

"I just can't deal with him at the moment. He is too in my face!" She called out as she ran for the bus which was heading to the gate. I would not be going anywhere yet. I needed to gather my thoughts. I dragged myself over to the canteen and sat, stirring a coffee for a while and dwelling on this awful set of revelations. I had to speak to someone. The only person it could be was my dad. Luckily, Max was still in the library, and I was able to grab a lift from him. As we drove home, I did everything in my power to keep quiet about Tess, and he spent much of that time quizzing me about her. I managed to put him at ease and convince him that she was just being a teenager, and there was nothing major going on. It made me uneasy that she wanted to block him from her life, though. Had he made a move on her? Had he tried something? It definitely wasn't his style. He was into Lisa and had been for ages. I dismissed those thoughts and arrived at dads. Funnily enough, he was out somewhere. He left a note to say he would be back by 11:00, and there was pasta in the fridge. I cooked it up and gave myself a sofa night, watching Netflix and drinking coke, trying my hardest to forget everything that was going on. Falling asleep next to the cat, Dad must have come back and covered me with a blanket, because I woke up again at around 3:00 in the morning and crept to bed. Just as I passed his room, a tall figure emerged, diving into the bathroom.

"Sorry Sam," he said.

"No worries," I replied as Matt darted past.

No worries indeed, I thought as I tried to make myself disappear, embarrassed by the complete surprise plastered across my face. This was the first time he had stayed over. I really needed to sleep at Mum's place when this was happening. I wasn't ready to be seen condoning their relationship. I didn't judge them for being gay, but he was still a married man. His wife would be at home, missing him, while he was having fun and games with my father.

Chapter 21 (Max)

Whilst Mum was out, I was struggling to get my iPad to connect to the printer, so I decided to try and see if I could print my homework out on her computer instead. She kept it in her room, and I wasn't sure if she used it much, but I knew that the password would probably still be the same as before; so I opened her door and had a look. Shrouded by a couple of skirts that she had dumped on top of the keyboard, Mum's computer looked as if it hadn't been touched in months. I switched it on and opened up a screen where I could type in the password. 'BradPitt20' still worked and made me chuckle, as she had always had an obsession with him. I myself had not seen any of his films and didn't know what all the fuss was about. Anyway, while trying to find the printer settings, I accidentally opened her emails up. Trying to close them again, I flicked the arrow which took you to the earliest messages in her box. This turned out to be the worst move for me to make. It led me to witness something that totally spun my world upside down.

I was shocked to see that the oldest messages in her box were from Michelle, Alfie's mum. I could not believe my eyes as I scanned a screen consisting only of message threads between the two of them. To me, what made this all the more surprising was that I never knew they were even friends. Perhaps there was something in these emails that gave a clue as to why Michelle had done what she did. Maybe she had confessed her feelings to my mum. I took a sharp intake of breath and opened one of the messages to find out more.

It read:

"Hannah,

If you do not stop harassing me, I will report you to the authorities. You have no right to treat me like this. I have always done what you asked of me. Leave me alone!"

Horrified, I opened the preceding message from Mum, which said:

"Michelle, you little bitch. Why are you still here? You should have left by now. Nobody likes you here, and you know that's the case. Leave the village and go somewhere you can make a fresh start. As a kid, you were always a walking disaster, and now you are just hanging around like a bad smell!"

I had never felt so uncomfortable before. This had come as a total surprise to me. Why were Mum and her arguing? Why was Mum being so mean to her? I read another one from Mum.

"You know you don't deserve happiness. That day when you hurt me will always be there, reminding me of what a cow you are."

Michelle replied:

"I didn't hurt you on purpose. You chose to stand on the back bar of my bike. It was out of my control. It was an accident, but you won't let me forget it."

On and on these emails went, arguing about things that had happened when they were kids. Sometimes the things were trivial, and sometimes they were not so trivial; but it certainly seemed like Mum had a sort of controlling influence over her, and she felt she was somehow in Mum's debt.

I rang Sam. I had to. He came over straight away, and we sifted through these reams of messages. We both sat there for ages, stunned by what we saw. I knew that Mum was out until at least nine o'clock, so we were in no rush to get through them. Every now and again, we stopped and discussed what we had read. My stomach developed an ache as I physically reacted to the realisation that my own mother was a bully. There was no question that she was the hateful one here. I made a copy of some of the messages onto a memory stick, and we closed down the computer, replacing the skirts so that Mum didn't know we had been in there. My essay seemed to take a back seat as we debated how to move forward. I loved my mum to pieces, but this did not make sense. She could not be like this! I packed a bag and walked to my auntie's place, with Sam in tow. I had texted Mum to say that Dad needed help with something. Knocking on Nicole's door, I hoped that he would be there, and Sam and I could explain what we had found.

He wasn't. Of course he wasn't. He was at the gym apparently, and so Nicole took us in and fed us while we waited. She tried to find out why we were so flustered, and we made up a story about having a tough time with school work. Offering to help, Nicole got quite frustrated when we said that wouldn't be necessary. She was after all a first class business graduate. The lawyer in her was inquisitive to the extent that we felt we were being interrogated by a prosecution. Eventually we both caved in a bit.

"OK. What we are going to tell you is massive. I mean, you cannot tell a soul."

"I am a top class aunt and brilliant at keeping secrets," she said, leaning into us a little.

"We found some e-mails. They are a bit delicate. We don't know what to do with them," Sam continued, taking over.

"What sort of emails? You found them? Lying in the gutter?"

"It was by chance that I found them," I said, implicating myself to protect Sam.

She insisted that I showed her them. Plugging the memory stick into her laptop, Nicole sat there glued to them, while Sam and I looked at the news on the telly. Apparently a hospital had been closed due to an outbreak of a serious infection.

"That must be a pain in the butt," he said as we then saw news that wild fires had burned their way across some parts of Middle America.

"Blimey, it's all going on," I tutted.

Nicole put her head up from the screen and cleared her throat.

"God, this must really make you feel like crap!" she suddenly announced, looking at me.

"To be honest, I don't know how to feel anymore. I am kind of numb to it all," I replied, honestly.

"You know, I was in the same class as both of them during secondary school, and I didn't know about any of this. We didn't hang out or anything, but you would have thought I'd have noticed some tension between them," she went on.

"What do we do now?" Sam asked, impatiently.

"Well, I am not sure if you read all of the messages but a few of them are about your dad. It is almost as if it all started with Michelle showing an interest in him. It suggests that she made a move on him when your mum was already starting to see him. I am not sure we should bring this up with Matt straight away."

We both looked at each other with blank expressions.

"He is coming back now, so I am going to copy these and shut down the laptop. Time for me to go to bed, as I have clients to meet early in the morning. I have a made-up bed in the spare room, Alfie. Sam, you are more than welcome to stay if you let your mum know."

At that, she gathered some of her things up and told us that she would sleep on it and decide what course of action to take the next day.

Dad came in and was happy to see me. He made us a drink each and then drove Sam home, with me in the car. When Sam got out, I moved into the front seat, and he told me about his night in the gym. Somehow he avoided asking me the real reason that I had showed up that late on a Tuesday night. He seemed genuinely pleased to see me. We played a game on the console and then went to bed. Tomorrow I knew that Nicole would come up with a way forward. She had to!

Chapter 22 (Alfie)

Heading to the post office a few days later to send off my passport application, I found it hard to find a parking space. Town was busy, and everyone seemed to have forgotten how to park. One car was at a really strange angle and took up almost three spaces. Another had blocked some cars in, and one of their owners was writing a snotty note out to stick on the window. I just couldn't seem to catch a break. Eventually I parked right down by the river and walked into the centre, squelching through puddles on the way.

When I got there, an old lady soon came over to speak to me. She didn't look as if she worked there, so I was slightly freaked out at first. What did she want from me?

"Hello young man, you have grown up no end," she began with a very soothing voice.

"Hello, I am really sorry, but I don't remember you."

She looked me up and down and said, "You look just like your mother."

Figuring that she must have known Mum, I eased up a bit and was happy to talk for a moment.

"She was an angel. A real, true angel," she continued kindly. "Every week, she made up food packages and sent them to a care home across the county. It was the one that your gran used to be in before she died."

Realising that she worked there after all, I asked her how she knew. She soon explained that her and Mum had chatted most days, and she was always coming in to drop off her parcels. It was so sweet to hear that Mum had done that. Such a charitable act. I felt so proud as she spoke of Mum, as though she were a hero. The lady commented on my dimples and then warned me never to do drugs. I smiled as I thought about the weed that I had been smoking just 20 minutes previous. Hoping that the chewing gum and spray had disguised the smell, I thanked her for her thoughts, dropped off my passport forms and made my way back to the river.

"I just saw your little sister!" yelled a familiar voice from across the way. It was Mrs Bellamy. I had not seen her for years. She still looked the same as ever. Her smart dress and expensive glasses always made her look stylish.

"Oh, what was she doing?" I called back.

"Sitting by the river over there!" she pointed as we crossed paths, with me on one side of the road and her on the other.

"Thank you! I hope everything is OK with you," I shouted.

"You too, dear," she replied before scuttling off.

It cheered me up to have had two nice things happen. First, meeting Mum's post office friend and now seeing my old head teacher. I went to try and find Tess, but there was no sign of her when I arrived.

Later that day, we were going to all go and watch Max in the school play. I had planned to get me, Tess and Dad a take-away beforehand. Tess had other ideas. She texted to say that she had plans with Minty, her slightly gothic friend. It didn't stop us going though. Dad and I ate our food and made our way over to the school theatre to make sure we got good seats before everyone else arrived. The charity this year was to do with anxiety and depression. Both Tess and Dad had championed this with the committee, and so Dad had been asked to say a few words after the play and thank the actors and director. Obviously this subject was close to our hearts, and we expected that tonight's play was going to be a tear jerker, especially as this week represented the ten year anniversary of Mum's passing. We sat fairly close to the stage, and I could see some of the actors, including Max, marching up and down behind the scenes, probably going over their lines for the last time and getting to grips with their nerves. I remembered with shame how I had ruined Max's first play back in primary school, and I wanted him to know how proud I was of him now, so I texted him to spur him on a bit.

Sam came in with his dad and sat a few rows back from us. Mrs Bellamy arrived with her husband, meaning that I had seen her twice in one day after hardly setting eyes on her for about seven years. Max's mum came in just before the lights went down and sat alone, looking serious and stoic.

The auditorium went dark. The music started softly. This was going to be Max's big night!

Chapter 23 (Sam)

Here we were sat, about to watch Max perform, and his aunt Nicole had still not got back to us about what to do next. The last thing she had said was that we needed to wait until the anniversary of Michelle's death had gone past. Tonight, it came to the front of my thoughts because I could clearly see Hannah sitting there in the front row, with her eyes fixed on the stage. I remembered how rude she had been to Michelle and started to feel enraged at everything she had done. I wished I could get up and go over there and have it out with her in front of everyone, but I restrained myself and ate some popcorn instead. Dad whispered to me that Matt had just slipped in on the other side of the room. I should have known that Dad would be looking out for him.

Before I switched my phone off, a message flashed up from Tess on my lock screen. I thought about opening and reading it but quickly decided against it, as the lights were dimming, and Dad nudged me to indicate that the show was beginning. I sat back, crossed one leg over the other and waited excitedly to cheer my friend on. Fingers crossed, he would rise to the challenge and show off the talents that we all knew he had.

Lisa came on first, performing well and making us all laugh with some well-placed gags. She was a shining star from the start and really seemed very comfortable up there on stage, with the lights glaring at her. The other characters were interesting and varied. Duncan was finding it hard to hit the spotlight every time; and Jane was sometimes pausing awkwardly, which I guessed was not simply for dramatic effect. But it was when Max arrived that the spotlight seemed to intensify. He was in the background of the scene to begin with, watching Lisa going on and on about something. Then it was his moment. He surged forwards and delivered his first lines crisply. He began a heated conversation with John and started to get into character comfortably. I was so proud of him as the story unfolded, and he had his own opportunity to get laughs from the audience. In moments of tension, he was electrifying. Even though he was my best friend, it was clear to anyone that he and Lisa owned the show. They captivated us, and Dad whispered to me that he felt they both deserved Olivier Awards. It sounded ludicrous, but I firmly believed they would have done equally well in any West End production.

They all took their applause; first one by one and then as a group. I cheered so loudly for Max that Dad leaned away slightly as if to say that his ears were about to fall off. A few wolf-whistles could be heard from Alfie and the others. We were all so excited because the play had been uplifting and overall the actors had done a brilliant job. As the noise died down, Alex was seen to walk towards the stage, where he took his position next to a microphone. Suddenly the general tone became more sombre.

The emotion in his voice was heavy; and even from where I was sitting, it was clear that his lip was quivering as he thanked the cast and crew for a delightful night's entertainment. He came onto the fact that it was all for a charity close to his heart, and then I suddenly got distracted. I had opened the text ready to read, and Dad leaned over me and pointed to it with despair.

"What the hell is she going on about?" he whispered loudly.

"Shh! Calm down!" I replied as I noticed the message's content.

It read: "Hannah is a bitch who needs to pay for her actions. I have had enough of this shit. She needs to pay. She will pay tonight!"

"Are we talking about Hannah over there?" he asked, trying to make sense of it.

"Yes, Dad, it seems that way."

"Psst!" Came another loud whisper, this time from Max, who was standing at the end of our row, beckoning me to join him. His wide smile had turned into a distressed appearance. I could tell she must have sent him one too. I tried to sneak out quietly, but with Dad following me, we were soon noticed by almost everyone. Alex looked up from his speech to shake his head at us.

Getting into the cloakroom, Max showed me his phone.

"Your mum is a bitch. I am going to make her pay for what she did!"

The message had stunned him, and he now was close to tears. I was in a panic as I considered the possibilities. What was she going to do?

It didn't take too long for us to find out. Max's mum appeared from nowhere and grabbed his hand, insisting that they had to leave immediately.

"I have just had a phone call from Ruby next door. She has been trying to call me for a while. There is a fire at our place. We have to go now!" She sort of screamed as she broke out into an almost running pace.

I looked at Dad, and he shrugged his shoulders. We turned towards the exit and raced towards our car. We had to find Tess before she got into any more trouble. God knows what she had already managed to do.

Chapter 24 (Max)

Driving up to our house, we could see a fire engine and ambulance parked outside, and a few men in high visibility jackets roaming around in the front driveway. Ruby came over to meet us and led us into the back garden. An ambulance man was stooped over a teenage girl, who I immediately recognised as Tess. Mum screamed as she spotted that our shed was half-burned to the ground, smouldering at the bottom of the long, dark garden. Tess looked away, loudly sucking on the oxygen mask that she had attached to her face. The ambulance man asked me to keep my distance for the time being, but Sam soon swooped past me and sat beside her, stroking her hair.

"What is going on here?" Mum whined.

"She was trying to get away, and she tripped over that tree stump in the dark," Ruby said, with a serious tone to her voice. "The little brat was lucky not to break a leg."

"I don't get it! What was she trying to do?" Mum replied, looking at me for answers.

I pulled her away from Ruby and decided to give her an honest answer.

"She wanted to hurt you!" I said, with a mixture of resentment and discomfort.

"Hurt me?"

"I know what you did, Mum. I saw your e-mails. I don't know how Tess found out, but you can bet she did this because she knows you bullied her mum."

For the first time in my life, I saw Mum break down in front of me. Like a chocolate bar sitting close to an open fire, she melted into tears and sniffles.

"That is not how it was," she squealed as Dad tapped me on the shoulder, asking me if I was alright.

"Listen to me. I was not bullying her. We used to be friends…but she and I just always argued."

Tess had stood up now and walked over to where we were standing.

"You are an evil cow who made my mum's life a misery!" she yelled, with one foot forward, and her left hand firmly clutching Sam's. You could tell that she was feeling vulnerable and needed back-up.

"Your mum hurt me one day. We were arguing outside the shops, next to that hill that leads down to the river. She was angry that I had got pregnant with Matt."

"When you were going to have me?" I asked, curiously.

"No!" interrupted Dad, "not you son."

Now I really was puzzled. I had no idea they had another child. My head began to spin, and I felt a supportive hand cross my shoulder and sling around onto my chest. Realising it was not Dad's, I looked to see who it belonged to. It was Lisa of all people. I was overwhelmed that she had made the effort to come and find me, but things were becoming more chaotic; and Alex and Alfie suddenly rushed in, with Tess flinging herself upon him.

"She killed Mum!" she shouted at the top of her lungs. "She bullied Mum until she could not face living anymore."

Alex swung around to us and asked, "What is all of this about?"

"Tess got a bit upset and started a fire in the garden here," said Sam, trying to remain calm.

"You told me you were out with your friends," Alex said to Tess, peeling her off him so the ambulance man could return the oxygen mask to her face.

"She really needs to rest now," he said, leading her away towards the ambulance.

Alfie went with them, but Alex remained behind for a moment to quiz Mum a little.

"Did you and Michelle have an argument?" he asked.

"We had many arguments, Alex!" boomed Mum, through a sprinkling of tears which immersed her cheeks. "We had always been friends, and then we fell out. Then we made up again. We were like chalk and cheese. We hurt each other many times over the years. But it was when she pushed me down that hill. That broke our relationship forever. There was no going back!" she whimpered, looking at Alex for some kind of appreciation.

He didn't give her any and seemed none the wiser.

"Pushed you? Michelle? Well, it must have been an accident," he cried.

"She knew what she was doing…and later that day, I lost my baby. I lost what was to be my first-born child because of her!"

"I can't handle this right now," squirmed Alex as he headed off to catch the ambulance before it drove away.

I took Mum's hand, and we went into our house. Dad put the kettle on, and Sam plonked himself down on the couch. Josh stayed outside with Lisa for a bit to help with the clear up and take a handover from the fireman. Mum stood staring at a photo of me, her and Dad when I was younger. She turned to me and smiled, still washed out but seeming less tyrannical and more like the mother I remembered in the past.

"Sometimes girls fall out when they are teenagers. But then they are pulled together again. I suppose me and Michelle had a kind of love/hate relationship. I think we always had had."

Everyone was silent, and the noise outside seemed to dissolve as she continued to speak about her side of the story.

From underneath the wine cabinet, she produced an envelope that I had never seen before. It was white and stamped with our address written on by hand in beautiful handwriting. Mum unravelled it and started to read it aloud.

"Dear Hannah,

When you read this, I will be long gone. I know that is what you wanted. I know it is for the best. I cannot live with myself for what I did to you. I have tried so many times to apologise and make up for it, but you have always told me to stay away and keep out of your life.

I have never been at peace since I pushed you, knowing that your baby died because of my stupid actions. I am so ashamed that I did such an awful thing, especially as all we were arguing over was Matt.

We were 17. I know age isn't an excuse, as I have said many times, but I didn't know what I wanted back then. Yes—I was jealous that you had the captain of the football team. He never even so much as looked at me apart from that one night at that dreaded barbecue, where you caught me trying my hardest to chat him up. I have admitted all of this.

I soon discovered the wonderful Alex. The moment he moved to our school, I knew he was the one for me. I had no hard feelings towards you, but you would not let it rest. I had no idea you were pregnant that day when I pushed you. But yes—I did push you. I was the reason for the death of your child. Despite every effort, I can see why you hate me so much.

Well, after this, you will never see me again, but know one thing. I have nothing but respect for you. You dealt with your loss so well. You are strong and confident, and we all admire you. Look after Max and Matt. Have a good life.

Michelle x"

We were all totally dumbfounded. I threw my arms around Mum, and we cried with relief. Relief that everything was making some kind of sense now. Dad said that he was sorry for hurting her, and he understood now the torment that she had been going through. Sam went off into the garden to relay it all to Josh. Everything was calming down a little. I asked Dad to swing past the hospital and explain everything to Alex, Tess and Alfie, as I knew he would be going there anyway. He was always so caring. He kissed me on the forehead before he left, and Mum and I were alone once more. We switched on the telly and had hot chocolates. For the first time in ages, we felt close again. It was lovely to think that now this was all off her chest, she could move on with her life, and I could have my wonderful Mum back.

Chapter 25 (Alfie)

Seeing her sat up and chirpy in the hospital chair made me feel so much better about what had happened. I hated the thought of my little sister harming herself. Feeding her some grapes, until she spat one out at me, I tried to make her laugh, but she was still a bit down. Dad had just relayed to her the full story which Matt had earlier delivered in the hospital foyer.

"I think you can safely say that none of this is Hannah's fault. Nor is it your mum's. Your mum was unwell. I mean we found all of those depression tablets afterwards; didn't we? I told you about that. Mental health can be an awful illness," he said as he tried drawing it to a close.

Tess nodded to show that she understood everything he had mentioned.

"Let's move on now, Tess. Mum would have wanted us to," I said, trying to sound supportive.

She nodded again and sat between me and Dad, drawing us together in a family huddle. It was great to know that we hadn't lost the closeness that we had always had.

Part Three – The Anxious Ghost

Chapter 26 (Michelle)

My mind was somehow sublime as I gently used the razor to cut a delicate line across my wrist that morning. The bath water was warm and soothing, but the pain struck me rapidly. I thought of how much I wanted myself gone. I wanted to be out of everyone's way. I wanted to escape a world I had always felt lost in.

The only friend I had ever cared about hated me. The husband I had loved so much had become distant. My children were joys to watch over, but I felt they deserved a far better mum.

Having just posted the letter to Hannah, I felt like I had done everything I needed to and knew that Tess would understand my grief many years later when she read my notes.

Friends can turn into bullies, and Hannah, for me, was a torment. She refused to forgive me. Her rejection was more painful than any vindictive act. Every time she glared at me or called me a bitch, she cut me somehow internally. I knew that her child had been lost because of me. I knew that she would never be able to look me in the eyes again.

Growing up with depression and having medication for many years made all of this so much worse. I had kept from Alex my secret, the anxiety that had cramped my youth. At first, Hannah had helped me no end. Her friendship as I grew up meant the world to me. It was like sugar in that; it fed my happy brain, leaving the demon side neglected for a while. But every time we fell out, the dark side ate away at me again.

Anxiety can destroy you. It had definitely destroyed me.

She was not to blame for any of that. But was it too much to be forgiven? By this time I knew that even if she did forgive me, I could never have forgiven myself for what I had done.

As I closed my eyes, I remembered all of the happy times we once shared. I was at peace with myself.

Now, looking down at my own grave, I am surprised by the bunches of flowers that engulf it. Alex regularly clears it up and makes sure it looks presentable. Alfie often pops by and tells me about what he has been up to. But it is right now, as I relay this to you, that I am most astonished by what I see, looking down on that graveyard, shrouded in morning mist.

I can see a teenage girl and a grown woman kneeling beside my grave. As they look at the carvings, I can clearly note those bright blue eyes of my daughter, Tess. She is tearful but speaks to me a little about how much she misses me and loves me. She has grown into a clever, sophisticated, independent young woman. My heart would burst but for obvious reasons…well, you know.

Next to her the woman reveals her face to be that of Hannah. She speaks to me about how much she regrets our arguments and tells me that deep down she has always adored me. Those words do it for me. They make it alright. Everything is as it should be.

Standing behind them I see Matt, in a tight embrace with Josh. I am proud of them for coming out and bravely showing the world that they love each other. My husband stands just beside them, smiling and holding onto a dog. A new edition to the household. I love knowing that he is happy again. Alfie kicks a ball around, trying to entice the dog to join in. He calls out towards me, "I love you, Mum."

So, there it is. I am never sure whether I should have done it. I can't go back now. But at least everything has settled. I wonder where their futures will take them.